WHISPERS
OF RUIN

THE OBSIDIAN ORDER DUET, BOOK 1

M.C. FITZ

ISBN: 979-8-89965-927-0
First Edition: June, 2025
Published by M.C. Fitz
Cover Art by MissFitz Design

Table of Contents

Trigger Warnings

Extreme Violence & Gore

Detailed murder scenes, torture, mutilation, branding, graphic injuries.

Sexual Assault

Non-consensual touching, coercion, harassment.

Toxic Relationships & Manipulation

Power imbalances, obsession, possessiveness, jealousy.

Psychological & Emotional Abuse

Gaslighting, threats, degradation.

Dubious/Missing Consent

Sexual encounters with blurred or absent consent.

Murder & Death

On-page killings, assassinations, execution-style deaths, described and detailed death.

Abduction & Captivity

Kidnapping, forced confinement, physical restraint.

Torture

Physical, emotional, and psychological.

Revenge & Vengeance

Violence driven by revenge, morally gray actions.

Criminal Organizations & Corruption

Secret societies, illegal activities.

Stalking

Monitoring, tracking, and invasion of privacy.

Self-Destructive Behavior

Recklessness, endangerment, risk-seeking actions.

Weapons & Knife Violence

Knives use, and other objects used as weapons.

Substance Use

Cigarette use, alcohol and altered states of mind.

Mental Instability

Characters displaying unhinged, obsessive, or sociopathic tendencies.

Consensual Rough/Dark Sexual Content

Degradation, impact play, possessive dynamics.

Morally Dubious Main Characters

Anti-heroes, villains as protagonists, blurred morality.

Blood Play

Use of blood in intimate or violent contexts, including knife play, licking, or smearing of blood.

Use of Objects Not Intended for Sexual Activity

Involves the use of unconventional or non-traditional objects in intimate or coercive situations.

To my daddy.

Not the one fate gave me with a shrug and no quality control,
but the one I chose.
My *real* daddy.
The father of my children.
The man who cheers me on through every wild idea, every
meltdown, every "this-time-it's-different-I-swear" project.

Maxime Guimond.

The best man that ever existed.
Because of you, I'll die peacefully knowing I've known true
love—the big, messy, soul-shattering kind.
You are the light I hold onto when I willingly fling myself into
chaos.
Thank you for our beautiful boys, for your endless love and
attention
(even when I clearly don't deserve it, because I'm kind of a
brat), and most of all, thank you for choosing me, so I could
one day say,
"I made that man happy enough to put up with my shit
forever."

I love you—ferociously, obnoxiously, eternally.

To all the girls their fathers forgot, it's okay.

Xan's your new daddy now.

He kills people, not feelings.

But hey, at least he stays.

Chapter 1

XAN

eath was the first thing I ever learned.

Not the kind that came swiftly, with mercy. The kind I knew lingered, insidious. It seeped into the cracks of your soul, staining everything it touched, poisoning the air you breathed. It stole pieces of you, whispering in your ear as the last drops of blood trickled from a still-beating heart.

I was nine when I witnessed my first kill. The same night my soul abandoned my body, leaving behind nothing but a shell, hollowed out by something I was too young to name.

Lucian stood over the man, his shadow stretching long in the dim glow of the moonlight. His blade gleamed—serene, patient. He didn't rush. He never did.

"This is how you survive, Xan."

His voice was steady, like he was telling me something as simple as how to tie my shoes.

"You control them, or they will control you."

The man beneath him gasped, a wet, strangled sound. His hands clawed at Lucian's wrist, desperation blooming in his eyes as he choked on words he could not afford to say.

I should have flinched when the knife sank into his chest. Should have recoiled at the gurgling cry that ripped from his throat, at the way his body jerked before going still. But I did not.

Because I already knew.

Survival, in Lucian's world, was not a right, it was earned. That lesson never left me. The Ruler of the Order made sure of it.

By the time I was sixteen, I had proven myself more times than I could count. The kills blurred together—faces, names, lives reduced to nothing but echoes of their final, desperate pleas. Begging. Bargaining. Praying to a God that never answered.

At last, they all ended the same way: at my feet, wheezing for that last sorrow only the divine could grant. I told myself it was necessary. That I was built for this. Lucian said as much, and I believed him—because I had no one else to put my trust in.

Now, at thirty-one, I am one of the best assassins the Order has ever produced. A clean record. No loose ends. The perfect weapon, controlled from afar—the prodigy. A ghost in the shadows, feared but never seen, designed for precision and efficiency. However, a weapon doesn't ask questions. A weapon doesn't dream of being something else.

Lucian Voss was never really a father to me. He was never even a mentor, not in the way most would define the word. No, he was a sculptor, and I was just the clay—an orphaned child, molded by his hands into something lethal.

Saving me wasn't his goal. Compassion never factored into it. Lucian is a calculated man, always two steps ahead, and I was nothing but another instrument in his collection.

I learned quickly that by his side, there was no room for weakness. No space for indecision. And absolutely no tolerance for defiance. His rules were law. His expectations, absolute.

I was the perfect student. Silent. Obedient. Ruthless. I mastered every skill he demanded of me—combat, strategy, deception, manipulation. I executed every order without question. Never hesitated. Never faltered. I was his greatest creation.

I told myself that it was enough, because I did not know what it meant to want more. What it meant to live outside of blood and orders, outside of survival and duty.

A normal life? A family?

That was a foreign concept, a language I had never learned to speak. There were no moments of warmth, no fatherly advice. Only the mission. Only the kills.

I never asked for more. But deep down, in the darkest part of me—the part I refused to acknowledge—I think I might have wanted it. A different life. A different outcome. But you do not get to choose your fate in this world.

In *his* world.

———— 🐱 ————

The city hums beneath me.

I can smell the faint whiff of street food—hot dogs and roasted nuts—rising from a corner below. The air feels heavy, as if it has been holding its breath all day, thick with the humidity of a late summer evening.

It clings to the skin, sticky, like a promise that the night won't come easy. The temperature is dropping, still I cannot quite escape the heaviness of the moment. Not yet.

I adjust my position on the rooftop, balancing on the edge of a rusted ventilation duct. My eyes stay on her—the view, somehow, feels foreign.

There she is.

She stands inside the gallery, her fingers trailing the margins of a painting as though it might shatter under her touch. A small, cozy venue tucked between two overpriced cafes in this neighborhood. I can see the soft glow of the lights inside, reflecting off her smooth skin, and the faint outline of her curvaceous body as she steps back, studying the canvas.

It is almost picturesque, this tiny, insignificant life she leads.

From my vantage point across the street, hidden in the shadows of an apartment building, I can just make out the details of her sleek figure through the glass. The way her long red hair catches the glow, the slight sway of her hips as she moves gracefully. It is a painting come to life, expertly crafted in every detail.

I reach up and rub my neck, feeling the cool metal of my watch under my fingertips. I could be anyone right now—another anonymous face in the crowd, just like Mira—living a life that doesn't matter.

Except I am not. And *neither is she.*

It makes me wonder what it is like to live like this way. To have a place where you belong. To be part of something more than the chaos that has been my life since I was old enough to walk. Then again, that is just a fleeting thought. I exhale sharply, shaking it off.

She moves to the counter, wiping it down, probably getting ready for the closing hours. The buzz of the street swarms around her, only here—inside her little bubble—it is quieter. It's safe. An existence without shadows or blood.

Damn, that must be boring.

I look down at the gallery. Mira is moving toward the back, probably to grab her coat or something to shut down the place for the night. Her thoughts are far removed from the eyes tracking her every step.

Yet I will be here. Watching. Waiting. Controlling.

I pull my black mask back down as I settle into the darkness, the leather compressing and unyielding. It molds the sharp features of my face other than the mouth, erasing my identity, locking me into something darker. My breath hisses through the small gap near my nose, warm and shallow against the cold material.

It is suffocating, although I have never felt more alive. The weight of the mask is not just physical—it's the persona it demands.

A predator. A phantom. Always close, lurking.

I am Xan Hayes, and I was born for this.

Chapter 2

MIRA

The gallery is almost silent now, the last of the visitors long gone.

The only thing I hear is the soft sound of the air conditioning with the quiet click of my heels on the polished floor as I make my last round. I wipe down the counter for the second time, even though it is already spotless. The routine helps me clear my overthinking mind.

I check the clock—nearly 8:30 p.m. Julian texted me earlier, asking if I would be home soon. Always trying to control the uncontrollable.

Sighing, I walk over to the painting that has been on my mind all week, the one I have been agonizing over. A simple street I painted a long time ago.

I step back to take it all in—the brushstrokes, the colors, the story behind that dream I still do not quite understand. There is a subtle beauty in it that calms me and makes me forget everything else for a dear moment.

The light flashes, creating a shadow over the canvas, and I blink, pulling myself out of the trance. The nagging feeling that has been following me all day returns.

I shake my head, trying to dismiss the feeling. Still, the sense of being watched lingers, creeping from the dark corners of the room. I glance over my shoulder, half-expecting to see someone standing there, yet the place remains empty.

I breathe in deeply, trying to calm the rush of thoughts that have gathered in my mind. Even with a slow exhale, I cannot get rid of them—it is there, just under the surface.

My hand brushes the side of the counter, the action mechanical, as if moving through the motions will help me push this anxiety away.

Julian always tells me there is nothing, just my mind running wild... Though I am not so sure anymore.

I grab my fake black fur coat and lock the door behind me, stepping out into the cool night air. New York at this hour usually feels more oppressive, in a calming sense somehow. I make my way down the street. The unease stays with me, crawling up my spine, each step filled with the sense that something is poised to strike.

I shake the feeling off, focusing on the streetlights ahead. I keep walking, trying to get free of the nervousness gnawing. The lampposts flicker overhead as I pass one empty storefront after another. The usual comfort of the familiar neighborhood looks distant tonight, swallowed by the heavy silence.

I am halfway down the block when I feel it again—that shift in the atmosphere, a breath of air that has been sucked from the night. I keep moving, the awareness prickling at my skin, pushing me onward. My pace quickens instinctively. Then, as I round a corner, I nearly collide with someone.

He moves back just in time, barely making a sound. I look up, my breath caught in my throat, as I see a figure standing beneath the streetlamp—tall enough to loom over me, his features shrouded in the dim glow. A hood casts a shadow over most of his face and his hands are dressed in tight leather gloves, the kind worn by someone accustomed to concealing both touch and intent.

"Sorry," I mutter, pulse still uneven.

He stays silent. Just continuing walking, his steps eerily soft against the concrete. His presence haunts my mind long after he disappears into the night. The way he moved—effortlessly, a shadow stretched too thin. Almost becoming part of the darkness itself.

I shake off the thought and keep walking. Just another stranger in the city. Nothing more. And yet, the feeling of being watched clings to me like a second skin.

By the time I get home, my mind is a tangled mess. Chaotic, restless. Julian is waiting on the couch, his expression familiar. Stable. A stark contrast to the storm in my head.

I force a smile, even though it feels distant, watching myself from the outside. I want to be alone—to unravel the restlessness that followed me through the streets.

When he steps into the bathroom looking for me, I undress in silence. The moment my shirt slips from my shoulders, I flinch, my arms instinctively crossing over my chest.

Julian watches me, confused, mostly impatient. He unbuttons his jeans, the soft scrape of fabric against skin filling the space between us.

Before I can protest, he presses me against the wet shower wall, scalding water running down my back. His lips claim mine—urgent, demanding. Sadly, all I feel is the cold detachment settling deep in my bones.

The image of the stranger suddenly invades my skull. I know nothing about this mysterious encounter, nor the color of his eyes or the sound of his voice. Yet my imagination takes great pleasure in recreating the missing elements that helped form the growing goosebumps on my legs.

Julian's mouth moves lower, his breath hot against my throat. I am not feeling him though. I feel a gloved hand closing around my neck. Fingers tightening, letting my poor mouth gasping.

Julian's hard cock slides between my thighs. His body presses forward. But the sensation feels off. As if it is happening to someone else.

I have been struggling for a while to get passionate. Anxiety maybe, I don't know... He is getting tired of it, which is understandable.

The unsettling thoughts are flowing through my head while my movements start to get detached. I feel my mind flying away, so does Julian's patience. I can see his anger bubbling up, his jaw clenching, the muscles in his neck visibly tensed. His eyebrows furrow deeply over his eyes as he starts to growl.

"I've been more than patient with you."

"I know..." I say, just as my lip starts trembling. The hot water is still pouring, covering up my incoming tears.

"I will do better next time, I promise..."

Julian chuckles, getting more distant, clearly disappointed.

"Sure, babe. Sure..."

I begin to wash my red hair, crying softly and silently just as he pushes furiously through the glass door to get out into the cold bathroom.

I am so useless and incompetent. The same way I have been three to four nights a week for months now.

What kind of girlfriend am I if I cannot give him what he needs?

A *shitty one*, that's who.

Chapter 3

MIRA

I wake up slowly to the soft light filtering through the blinds. The apartment is quiet—almost too quiet. I swing my legs off the bed and sit on the border, my feet meeting the cool floor.

The discomfort from yesterday has not faded, the echo of someone watching me, although the rest of the apartment is empty.

I glance at Julian, oblivious to the tornado brewing inside me, the constant loneliness even when surrounded by the people I cherish the most. He would not understand anyway. He never does and kind of always takes things I say very personally.

Sighing, I make my way to the kitchen, hoping the routine of making coffee will calm me. The familiar smell fills the room, grounding my head. I almost feel normal.

Suddenly, the image of that man flashes in my mind again—the way he stood in the shadows, so still, so silent, so... commanding. I shake my head, trying to brush it off even if the thought stays, refusing to fade.

I close my eyes, breathing through the tension in my chest—and lower. No matter how much I tell myself to stop, there is a part of me that clearly does not want to. Because, in some strange and perverted way, that memory alone makes me feel more alive than I have felt for so long.

I open my eyes and pour the coffee, my hands steady despite the whirlwind in my head. I focus on the small, casual motions—the clink of the mug, the swirl of steam—trying to drown out the sensation of danger that still inhabits my mind.

Maybe today will be different. Maybe this feeling will finally fade.

Deep down, I know it won't.

I take a sip, trying to concentrate on the warmth of the beverage in my hands. The fridge is the only sound breaking the room. For a brief moment, I almost convince myself that everything is fine—normal, even.

That's when I hear it. A faint creak.

It surely is nothing... You're turning more paranoid than a chihuahua on espresso.

Just the apartment settling. Still, my grip on the mug clutches, I look toward the hallway. I set the cup down and force myself to check, you know, just in case. I walk through the apartment, opening closets and wardrobes. There is no sign of anything out of place.

When I return to the kitchen, a subtle knock makes me jump. My heart pounds as I glance at the clock—it is too early for visitors. Not that I ever actually have visitors—thanks to my sparkling social life and magnetic charm, of course.

I debate ignoring it, but the knocking continues, now sharp and insistent. Taking a deep breath, I walk through the hallway and peek through the peephole.

No one's there.

I open the door cautiously to find a package on the floor. It is small and meticulously wrapped in plain brown paper, with my name written in cursive letters in the middle, in dark crimson ink.

My stomach knots as I carry it inside. Setting it on the counter, I stare at it, half-expecting it to explode or to scream at me like the howler envelope did to Ronald Weasley in *Harry Potter*.

Julian's voice breaks the silence, groggy and muffled from the bedroom.

"What's happening?"

"Nothing, nothing," I call back, forcing steadiness into my voice. "Just a delivery."

I notice at the top—my name in clear, clean handwriting, the ink almost too perfect. No return address, no sign of who sent it. I ordered nothing. And I sure as hell do not remember asking for something, as if Julian Beckett would get it for me anyway.

My curiosity pushes me forward. I reach for the package; the paper crinkling under my fingertips as I carefully peel back the tape with the small green knife I keep in the drawer. I work my way around the edges, keen to see what is inside, the blade sliding smoothly under the surface. It is almost as satisfying as those ASMR carpet cleaning videos I tend to watch late at night, trying to quiet the recurring nightmares that haunt me.

Without warning, the knife hits something unexpected. I hesitate, thinking it is just the cardboard, but with a sudden sharp motion, the blade gives way, and I feel a hot sting across the side of my hand to my wrist.

"Damn it!"

The knife clatters to the floor as I pull my hand back. My skin is sliced open, a trail of blood immediately pooling at the surface. The cut is shallow, but it hurts and bleeds like hell. I pull my hand to my chest instinctively, my heart pounding.

"What in the actual fuck was that?" I mutter under my breath, my mind racing with frustration and confusion.

The sensation of the blade biting into my skin seems deliberate, as if the package was meant to hurt me. I grab a paper towel from the counter, pressing it against the wound to staunch the bleeding. My fingers shake slightly, my annoyance building.

I return to the package, the thought of what is inside suddenly feeling a little more ominous. I finish cutting the tape with more caution, but as I peel back the last flap of paper, I cannot help but feel a nagging suspicion that this container is wrong.

The box is full of crumpled tissue paper. At first glance, it seems harmless, even mundane. But while I dig through the soft layers, I pull out a folded sheet of paper—something is weighing it down beneath it.

I reach deeper and pull out a small, sharp object hidden among the tissues. It's a razor blade, its edges gleaming in the light. I freeze, my breath catching in my throat.

What kind of crazy sickos would do something like this?

My hand pulses with a dull ache as the sense of being watched grows back again. I push the paper and the blade aside to find... A sketch.

A detailed drawing of me in the gallery, the faint reflection of myself in the window capturing the exact moment I stood there the day before, lost in thought, right before closing.

I inspect the drawing, my pulse quickening for reasons I cannot entirely explain. The scene is too accurate, too precise to be a coincidence. That is when I notice it—scrawled in faint pencil along the bottom corner.

> *Nice view, huh? You should see the original.*
> *Here's some advice, Ginger. Don't paint yourself into a corner.*
> *PS: Here are some tissues for your hand.*
> *X -*

My chest contracts as I stare at the message. The pain in my hand suddenly seems secondary to the icy chill creeping up my spine.

Who the hell is X?

How do they know about me?

I consider for a second scream for Julian. *Oh no.* He will call the police and keep me hidden in my apartment forever.

I stare at the memo again, trying to make sense of it. The words feel like a warning, but for what? My mind flashes back to last night—the man in the shadows, his presence invading my head and body long after he had disappeared.

Could it be him?

I grab my phone, take a photo of the sketch and the note before tucking everything back into the box. My fingers hover over the screen, debating whether to call someone—Zoey, my best friend and coworker maybe?
Instead, I set it down.

Whoever sent this knows me, knows where I work, where I live. They wanted me to see it, to feel it. And as much as I hate to admit it, it's working.

I quickly grab a clean paper towel, pressing it to my palm to stop the bleeding. My hand trembles as I feel the burn of the cut, the skin still warm where the blade has sliced through it.

I run to the bathroom, pull open the medicine cabinet, and grab a big plaster. My fingers fumble with the small adhesive strip, and I curse under my breath as I press it to the cut.

The coolness of the bandage against my skin is a slight relief, still as I examine it in the mirror, something startles me. The sight of that fresh cut, the blood that has stained the white paper, suddenly feels like more than just an accident.

It is a reminder that someone wanted to get close enough to hurt me.

I stare at my hand, the weight of that reflection settling in my heart. A weird feeling pulses in me—I cannot quite explain what. It is almost as if I'm... grateful for it.

Someone wanted to make me feel something, to make me real, regardless of whether it was in the form of pain, which I do not normally enjoy.

It is twisted, I know. As I stand there, looking at my new mark, part of me feels a deranged sense of satisfaction. For a second, I feel noticed, alive, excited, and maybe even... loved. It feels like a window opening in my brain, revealing a still-dark room filled with echoes and possibilities of new experiences.

I realize there is a slight tension brewing in my lower body, a vibration that subtly shakes my inner thighs, an irresistible pull that stirs my desire to understand, to feel more. I study at my reflection in the cabinet mirror intently, trying to find some clue about what the hell is going on with me.

Without warning, the searing sensation of my injured hand sliding into the blue-laced panties completely takes me off guard. I maintain eye contact, surprised, as if that reaction might somehow release me from any guilt. I silently laugh.

The shame of complete arousal as my fingers penetrate my pussy, the blood creating a perfect lubricant. It's soft and velvety, almost like sinking into a thick cloud. While I move my hand with a gentle, smooth resistance, my insides slightly quiver as I go deeper.

The instant I proceed to a quicker, rhythmic pace, the mysterious, black hooded stranger consumes my mind once more. I grab my breast, my nails piercing my chest, imagining it is gloved and big. My eyes roll and a stifled moan slips from my muttering lips.

"You good out there?" asks Julian from the bedroom next door.

Holy crap.

34

I completely forgot he existed—that he was just beyond the wall, blissfully unaware of what was happening here. How could I do this to him?

He has been patient for months now while I stand here, masturbating with my fucking blood when I could have saved this rare instant of excitement for the man I am trying to build a life with.

I raise my head and profoundly examine my face with disgust in the mirror, taking in every detailed reaction, showing how eager I am to come. I know fully well that what I am doing is not right, yet I am so desperate for any escape, and for one brief, selfish moment, the sharp guilt is a reprieve from the dullness of everything else.

My hands still tremble as I go through the motions, a quiet voice in the back of my mind screaming for me to stop.

There will be no turning back.

Instead of listening to the voice of reason, clearly conscious of the precedent this could create, I carry on fantasizing about that enigmatic outsider who has nothing to do with my current situation.

What do I know about this guy? I almost crashed into him at the street corner.

Here go the wedding bells, am I right?

Damn, I am such an idiot. Getting caught up over some passing figure like a teenager with Edward Cullen. For all I know, he didn't even notice me. Just a brush of shoulders, a fleeting second in the city's madness.

The only thing I reckon is his smell. A scent so intoxicating, a complex blend of raw masculinity and subtle sophistication. It carried hints of cedarwood, smoky leather with a faint trace of something darker—remembering the embers of a smoldering fire. The aroma wrapped itself around me, warm and compelling, making it impossible to contain my orgasm any longer.

At last, a soothing feeling, comforting as the scarlet liquid mixed with my arousal floods onto my wrist, soft enough to feel like a luxurious embrace.

It is so delightfully wrong, as though the devil himself were attempting to worm his way into my soul, showing me just how every forbidden desire deserves to be explored.

When I finally pull my fingers out, the sanguine fluid slowly drips from my hand, leaving a contrasted trail of red drops on my white ceramic floor. It's a tactile, indulgent feeling.

Like my blood *finally* belongs to me.

Chapter 4

XAN

*L*ucian sits across from me, his usual calm arrogance steadfast in place, but I can feel the pressure behind it—the kind of calmness that is not meant to reassure, but to disarm. His office is as it always was—dimly lit, thick with his authority. He rests his elbows on the desk, steepling his fingers in front of his face as he studies me.

"Xan, my boy," he begins, his voice smooth and deceptively warm. "Didn't I tell you not to play with your food?"

I take my time, leaning back in my chair, crossing my arms, and stretching my legs.

"You gave me a job, and I'm doing it my way."

"Are you?", he tilts his head slightly, his piercing blue eyes narrowing. "Because from what I see, we are still incapable of telling what she knows. You have been watching her for weeks now." He spreads his hands, his tone almost amused.

I keep my expression neutral.

"You told me to watch, not act. I'm following orders."

His gaze sharpens, cutting through the space between us.

"For someone who's meant to stay hands off, you sure take your time toying with her."

He leans forward, his arms hitting the desk.

"What is it about her, Xan, *huh*?"

My jaw clenches.

"Nothing. She's a total nobody."

Every muscle in my body screams for release. My fingers curl tighter, nails digging into my palms as I fight the urge to snap. I stare at him, forcing myself to keep my expression neutral, but inside, I am a fucking storm.

The worst part? He can probably see it. The Ruler always knows when someone is on the brink. He clearly enjoys every second, thriving on the power he exerts over us all.

Lucian leans back, his eyes twitching into a faint, condescending smile.

"You have always been thorough. That's why I trust you more than anyone else.", he pauses. "Still let me remind you, boy—there is a fine line between patience and distraction."

I hold his gaze, refusing to let him see how deeply his words are cutting. How his voice can instantly ignite that searing anger boiling under my skin, clawing its way up my throat like acid.

I nod once, curtly. "I will keep watching. I will find out what she knows."

His tone now shifting back to something almost paternal.

"Good, good. That's what I need from you. Stay close to her. Earn her trust. Exploit her weaknesses. If she has no idea who I am, if the past remains buried, then maybe—*maybe*—she can still be of use."

He stands, walking around the desk and resting a firm hand on my shoulder.

"I made a promise to someone dear to me once—to welcome that girl within the great walls of the Order. Although I can't afford to keep that oath if she becomes a threat. I took you in because I saw potential, Xan. And you have never let me down. Don't start now, son."

His grip lingers a second too long before he steps away.

"So, keep her alive—*for now.* If she starts asking the wrong questions... I hope I won't have to tell you what to do."

———— *ℓ* ————

The heavy oak door of Lucian's office slams shut behind me, reverberating down the narrow corridor. The hallways of the Obsidian Order's headquarters are gloomy, intentionally oppressive, their stone walls whispering secrets of those who walked these paths before. Chandeliers hang precariously, their chains creaking faintly with every draft, casting erratic shadows that dance like restless spirits. My boots echo with each step, a steady rhythm that contrasts with the rage in my head.

The exit is right ahead—a towering iron door that groans as I push it open. Outside, the night greets me with a damp chill. The rain has stopped, leaving the cobblestone streets slick and gleaming under the amber glow of distant streetlights, blending with the fog that clings stubbornly to the ground.

I light a cigarette, inhaling deeply as I walk, the atmosphere quieter than it should be for New York, even in Vinegar Hill. The neighborhood has usually its own pulse, a thrum of life beneath the surface. Here—where the Order's influence stretches—it feels muted, almost lifeless.

Mira's apartment is not far, and I certainly do not fucking need Lucian to order me to keep an eye on her; I already made her my priority.

I crush the cigarette underfoot as her street comes into view. The gallery's faint light glimmers through the smog, drawing me in, whether or not I want it to.

Tonight, there is no need for a rooftop or a telescope—I want to savor every drop of her fear. I want to be close enough to see her blue-green eyes narrow and her legs tremble the moment she senses my presence. And according to the cameras I installed in her apartment, I can shock her pretty well.

Still working late this evening, Ginger?

Through the side bay window, I watch Mira pull her phone from her left pocket as it softly vibrates. She glances at the screen, her brows knitting in confusion, and starts looking around erratically, searching for something—or someone.

I think you got the wrong number.

She puts her cellphone back anxiously into the pocket of her blue jeans, which mold perfectly to her ass. I wonder what color her face would turn with my belt tightly circling her neck.

Do you?

I don't know who the fuck gave you my number, but leave me alone, freak!

A faint smile creeps onto my face—the girl's got some balls.

Is this how you always treat people who accidentally dial the wrong number?

From her expression, I can tell she's realizing I might actually be innocent, that she might have completely lashed out at the wrong person.

Sorry, but I'm clearly not the one you're trying to contact. My apologies once more.

I give her a moment to compose herself, letting her believe it might be over.

But of course, little fox, I'm not going anywhere. I'm the hunter, and you'll be forever my prey.

Chapter 5

MIRA

Right before closing the gallery's front door, my phone vibrates again. I freeze, a wave of dread washing over me. I can feel the panic rising deep within, my stomach twisting in knots.

I am literally on the verge of throwing up from the anxiety. I take a deep breath and look at the screen.

Oh my God, it's Zoey. It's only Zoey.

Feel like going out for a drink bestie? 😊

I cannot help to think that alcohol might actually be the answer right now.

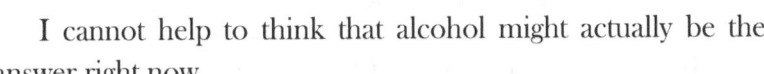

I might regret this... but where do you want to take me this time?

> Skyline, it's new and I heard it's filled with all the hottest guys in NY, and I ab-so-lu-te-ly need to get laid. Like this is a life-or-death situation, Mira.

I chuckle softly. Zoey always leaves me torn between rolling my eyes in exasperation or laughing so much my stomach hurts.

> Lol, you're so stupid, I'll meet you there. ♡

The second I step into the Skyline, the city seems to shrink below me.

The place is perched high above New York, with floor-to-ceiling windows that stretch across every wall, framing the glowing cityscape. With the smells of sweetened cocktails and leather upholstery, the kind that tells you everything here is polished, curated and expensive.

I make my way through the dimly lit space, my cherry red shiny heels clicking against the marble floors. Neon lights in soft pinks and blues buzz from the bar, reflecting off the mirrored surfaces, creating faint halos around everyone.

The crowd is alive, a mix of fancy suits and slinky dresses, each person sipping on glasses filled with colorful concoctions that look too pretty to drink. A soft, bass-heavy track pulses in the background, just loud enough to make my heart sync with it. I peek toward the bar—it is sleek, black granite with gold accents, the bartenders moving like choreographed dancers.

I head toward the far corner where the windows meet. That is where the real magic happens. The entire city sprawls out before me, lights stretching endlessly, their glow fighting off the night's darkness. It is breathtaking, overwhelming in its enormity.

I try to focus, to lose myself in the rhythm of beauty, but something still feels... eerie. My eyes keep drifting, scanning faces, corners, and shadows as if my body knows something my mind doesn't. I shake my head, laughing at myself.

"You're being ridiculous," I mutter, maybe it is just the strange energy of the night. Too many people, too many flashing lights. Yet, the tension curls low in my abdomen.

Then it happens again. That *feeling*.

Out of the corner of my eye, I catch a figure—tall, dark, and dominant—just standing there, watching. I whip my head around to look, but there is nothing. Just the crowd, a crush of bodies pressed together, all moving to the hard beat thundering through the room.

I smile nervously, brushing it off.

You are not Ted Bundy's next victim, Mira. Calm down.

Even as I try to convince myself, I cannot help but looking over my shoulder again. Before I can shake it off, someone steps into my space, too close for comfort. He smells like cheap cologne and vodka, and his grin is wide, way too wide.

"Hey, beautiful," he says, leaning in, his breath warm against my ear.

I take a step back, forcing a polite smile.

"Thanks, but I'm not interested. I have a boyfriend."

"Aw, come on," he presses, his hand brushing my waist. "He's not here, is he?"

I feel my stomach churn, my pulse quickening.

"Seriously, no. Please."

But he doesn't back off. His grip tightens, and I search around for Zoey in panic, for anyone, but the crowd is too thick.

And, like a fairy tale's cavalier on his black horse, *he* appears.

One second later, the guy is yanked away from me with a force that leaves me stunned. The next moments blur together. An imposing figure stands over the guy, his appearance obscured by his black hood and the flickering lights.

Without a word, he lands a punch so powerful that he sends the guy stumbling back on the floor. Another follows, and another, and another until I can't follow the count anymore. The mass parts slightly, gasps rippling through the air, although no one dares to step in.

I stand frozen, a soft tear rolling down my cheek, my chest heaving as I watch the scene unfold. The man is controlled, precise, and terrifyingly calm as he delivers one final blow. The other guy lies on the floor in a pool of his own blood, almost lifeless. His nose is completely broken, and there is a tooth lying next to his disfigured face.

Around him, shattered glass from a fallen drink scatters across the floor, while the bar's neon lights flash, casting shadows over the damp ground.

People gather around, some watching with curiosity, others indifferent, as if scenes like this are just part of the club's usual atmosphere. The music still thumps loudly, almost drowning out the murmurs rising.

The badly beaten man slumps to the ground, groaning in total agony, and the stranger straightens, rolling his neck, finally turning toward me.

Our eyes lock for the first time.

His face is hidden behind a black leather mask, the soft light reflecting over its edges. Yet, his presence is absolutely overwhelming. He doesn't speak, doesn't move—just watches me, his heavy breaths the only sound I can hear.

There is something utterly magnetic about him, something dangerous. My pulse races, a caged bird in my chest. I feel trapped under his gaze, unable to move or look away, mesmerized by the unsettling mystery of the man before me.

And, just like that, he's gone.

He disappears into the night as quickly as he appeared, leaving me standing there, breathless and trembling.

Who the hell was that?

It is as if he completely vanished, leaving behind only the memory of his presence: sharp, dominating, and absolutely terrifying. I stumble backward, my fingers digging into the corner of the bar for support, struggling to catch my breath. Zoey rushes to my side, her face pale even for her dark skin, her brown eyes wide.

"What the hell was that, Mira?" she whispers, shaking, barely audible over the chaos.

"I... I don't know," I stammer, still scanning all around, hoping—or maybe dreading—that I will catch another glimpse of him. "He just... appeared out of nowhere!"

Zoey's hand wraps around my arm.

"Do you think he knew that guy? Or you? Why would he do that?"

"I don't know, ok!" I say loudly as my stress stumbles dangerously close to its breaking point.

Something deep inside me feels like I know. Or at least, like I should. The intensity of his stare, the way he looked at me before disappearing—it was not random.

The room feels suffocating and I am about to scream, agonizing. A panic attack erupts, stripping away my ability to bring air into my lungs. I break down, tears flowing endlessly like a relentless stream on a stormy night.

"Let's get you out of here, poor thing."

Zoey pulls me into a warm embrace, pressing my head against her to shield me from the curious stares surrounding us. The warmth of her body offers a fleeting solace in the suffocating strain, and I cling to the familiarity of her scent, my fingers curling into the fabric of her shirt. Her steady, but quick heartbeat offers a rhythm to cling to. Even in her arms, I can't put away the feeling that my mind is slipping out of control.

Unaware of where I am going, I follow Zoey, the oppressive music from the bar fading more and more with each step.

Chapter 6

MIRA

I return home, barely conscious of my surroundings as I make my way to bed. I am not really sure how I got here, but I am so thankful Zoey was with me. Without bothering to change, I collapse into the sheets, exhaustion taking over, and I fall into a deep sleep almost instantly.

I wake up with the heavy feeling of a hangover, even though I did not drink a single drop last night. My head is pounding, my limbs weighty. As far as I know, *I* wasn't the one throwing down like some shirtless wrestling deity yesterday.

The atmosphere in my room is invading and stifling, as if time itself hesitates to intrude. For a moment, I stay still, staring at the ceiling, my mind tangled in the haze of sleep. But then— flashes.

The club. The fight. The *stranger*.

My pulse rises and I feel the panic attack taking control of my body once again. I can still sense the ghost of hands touching my arms, the press of unfamiliar bodies, flesh meeting flesh—the sound of his knuckles colliding with that guy's jaw.

It was not just a dream; it was a horrifying nightmare.

I really need to get out, to focus my mind on something else.

Julian is away again on another business trip, as usual. The idea of heading to the library to sketch crosses my mind, a way to escape solitude and bad thoughts. I do not let myself think this through while I jump out of bed to get dressed, grab a chocolate chip cookie, and head straight outside.

The bustle of the city fades behind me as I walk, the pressure of the world easing slightly, replaced by the calm that awaits in the quiet of the library.

When I finally arrive, I take a second to soak in the silence that surrounds me. It feels cooler inside, and the soft light filters through the rows. There is a particular scent in the air—dusty pages, the presence of pure knowledge.

I wander further into the aisles, letting my fingers brush the spines of the books, seeking the peace my head so desperately craves.

As I slip deeper into the labyrinth of bookshelves, my phone buzzes in my pocket, the sudden sound fulling a direct jolt to my system. I pull it out, relaxing as I know it is Zoey asking about last night.

Have you ever been fucked in a library before?

My eyes widen, going as round as marbles. I freeze. My heart stutters.

There is no mistaking that message this time.

I don't know who the hell you are, but stop following me or I'll call the police.

Would you rather have had the police save you last night?

Last night? How the hell could that person possibly know that? Unless...

I didn't need any saving.

Well, you will need some now.

A loud bang sounds in the distance, too close for comfort. I press my hands to my mouth to stifle the startled gasp that slips out, its echo fading in time with the reverberations of the earlier noise.

I quickly shove my phone back into my pocket, my legs moving of their own accord, urging me to get lost. I don't know why I'm running—I am not even sure what I'm escaping. I slide between the shelves, keeping it to the shadows, my breath shallow as I press my back against the cool books and sit down to hide.

Every small sound around me feels amplified, my pulse a steady drumbeat in my ears. I try to keep quiet, but a voice in my head tells me it is futile.

He is coming.

Another buzz.

I'm getting closer.

That's when I hear it—the unmistakable footsteps resonating through the aisles. Slow. Methodical. I can feel him drawing closer like the predator he is. I get up hurriedly and round a corner, and all of a sudden, I am not alone anymore.

He's there.

Standing in the narrow passage between the shelves, his presence overwhelming. He doesn't say a word, just steps forward, and before I can react, his hand closes around my wrist, yanking me toward him.

"You thought you could run," he murmurs, his voice a low growl. His hold intensifies, and I feel the heat of his body against mine.

My heart skips a beat. Fear, excitement, and something darker swirl inside as I try to understand what is going on.

I attempt to pull away, but he does not let go. His other hand presses hard against my neck, just enough to make me gasp for air, still not enough to choke me. The adrenaline has my blood pumping faster, every nerve in my body is on high alert.

"Do not think you can ever escape me, little fox. Because I will always hunt you."

My chest heaves loudly beneath the weight of his touch. I lift my head abruptly, our stares lock in a silent battle. Mine shimmer with unshed tears, while his, behind his mask—hazel, pale, and eerily piercing—keep me captive. So light, yet impossibly dark—the perfect contradiction.

He yanks my wrist toward him, the bruising pressure of his fingers still burning against my skin. He pulls up just a bit his mask, his lips parting slowly, filled with both hunger and intent, before his tongue meets my flesh.

Heat and moisture trail up my arm as he licks, his mouth closing around my fingers. Just as abruptly, he lets go—a faint *pop* echoing as my hand slips free from his grasp.

"Looks like only one of your hands had the privilege of being properly marked by that box the other day. How about we fix that, *hmm*?"

Terror floods my body and seizes my heart. I steal a quick look at my other hand, still wrapped in the bandage Zoey had carefully applied the other day. It had taken all my effort to convince her I had simply cut myself while chopping carrots.

What lie would I have to come up with this time? That I had been practicing for a *Five Finger Fillet* tournament? Because nothing says "well-adjusted adult" like willingly stabbing the table between your fingers for fun...

"Don't you dare..."

My sentence is abruptly cut short as my breath is stolen from me.

"*Tut tut*, silence my sweet little foxling or I will fucking break your pretty neck." He stops and pulls closer. "Not only will you lose your ability to breathe, but you won't be able to live at all."

I bite back the rest of my words, wisely choosing not to finish my sentence. My legs tremble as the color drains from my face, leaving it a deep shade of purple. My vision blurs as I can feel myself slipping away. He loosens his grip for just a split second before I lose consciousness, letting out a small, malevolent smirk.

"I want you wide awake as I bestow upon you the gift of being branded." The words hit me like a slap.

'*The gift of being branded*', like I was some damn livestock.

"You belong to me now, and we need to make sure everyone knows it." *What the fuck that freak is talking about?*

He lets go of my neck and pulls out a lighter, along with another small object from his pocket, one that I cannot quite make out.

"You know, when a farmer receives a new shipment of cattle, he marks them to identify his belongings properly."

I hear the lighter clicking.

"Personally, I think it is more about claiming his territory, ensuring no one ever steals what is in his possession." He sighs in satisfaction. "And that's exactly what I intend to do with you."

The pain is instant and searing as he burns a clean 'X' across my forearm with some kind of seal. I gasp, the sting making my whole body tense, yet sending an unexplained exciting shiver through me all at once.

"Can you feel it, Mira? Do you feel the shockwave of pain coursing from your arm to your pussy?" His hand delicately caresses my shoulder. "The pure agony that consumes you like nothing has ever shaken you before," his fingers sliding on my breast and falling to my waist, right through my pants.

"You are completely deranged," I breathe, trembling from head to toe.

He pulls his face closer, eyes burning beneath the mask. "Then tell me to stop."

It's not a request. It's a dare.

I swallow hard. "You wouldn't listen anyway."

His laugh is low, dangerous. "Exactly."

"That's fucking insane," I snap, trying to stay steady.

He tilts his head, voice dark with heat.

"And yet, you are soaking through those panties."

Suddenly, it hits me—that scent. I could recognize it among a thousand. It had wrapped around me like a whisper just days ago, embedding itself deep in my memory. A blend of warm spices and whiskey, laced with the faintest trace of smoke.

Oh my God...

It is *him*, it has been him from the beginning.

His hand hovers over the glistening slitted junction between my thighs and I can tell by the look in his eyes through the leather mask that he's smiling right now—proud and satisfied.

"Do you realize how fucking wet you are, Mira?", he says with his deep and hushed voice. "Even more than when you fucked yourself with the blood I provided for you, just like the perfect deviated girl you are."

I cannot deny it. I honestly had never been this turned on in months and I cannot figure out how or why.

"Please stop," I plead. "I have someone in my life, as you clearly know by now..."

He glares at me, his anger palpable.

"I am scorching your arm as if you were some kind of lowlife slave, and the thing you really fear is that boyfriend of yours?" Without thinking, I retort.

"It is not fear, it is call love. Something I'm guessing your mother never bothered to teach you!"

I instantly regret my answer as I feel a biting, swift slap across my face, so sudden that it leaves me momentarily dazed. The searing pain electrifies my skin, nearly knocking me off balance. I grit my teeth, my eyes squeezing shut feeling the tears well up, threatening to spill over.

His fingers close around my jaw, forcing my head back with a hand that feels like steel. The strain of his arm is suffocating, and I can't move, can't escape. A wave of helplessness washes over me as I am trapped under his unyielding brutality.

"Let me teach you real love then."

He swiftly snatches a magazine from the table beside me and rolls it up tightly. I am choking in an ocean of terror, trying to figure out a way to get out of here and realizing there is no possibility of evading whatsoever.

In a fury, he tugs my pants down, stripping me away with a single, ruthless pull. The masked man throws me one last feral look before thrusting, without any warning, the rolled-up magazine sharply into my pussy, the impactful force causing it to split open with an excruciating suffering. The tears I had fought so hard to restrain begin to spill down my flushed cheeks.

I cry silently, too stunned by the situation to make a sound. I can feel the firm pressure of his cock against my belly.

He pulls my legs up, positioning them on each side of his waist. My back slams against the wall with such power that the shelves shudder and books crash to the floor in a chaotic clatter. The pages crumble, tearing lightly into my flesh, leaving behind a trail of severe pain.

Simultaneously, the tip drives farther, pushing me to the edge of the unbearable, fueling a surge of wild euphoria. A war rages within me. Every rational part of my mind screams that this is wrong, that I should be disgusted, terrified—anything but this. And yet, my body betrays me for a darkness temptation.

I want to blame him. I want to convince myself that this is manipulation, that he has twisted my desires into something I would have never wanted on my own.

But the truth is far worse.

Because I do want this. Not just the act itself, but the way it makes me feel—powerless, yet exhilarated, humiliated, yet seen. There is something intoxicating about the way he controls me, the way he strips away my walls without permission.

Am I sick? Broken? Or is this just a part of me I have refused to acknowledge until now? The thought should repulse me, but it only ignites the fire he has already set within me.

With a sharp tug, he grabs my ponytail, yanking my head back. His hot breath grazes my face as he leans in, his lips dangerously close to my ear.

"Tell me, little fox, that you are not feeling loved right this second, and I will call you the worst fucking liar to have ever existed.", he murmurs, his low, haunting voice slipping under my skin like an uncontrollable shiver.

"How... How can you even talk about love?", I shoot at him crying uncontrollably. "You act like a total savage and yet, you dare talk about love?"

He lets out a small sarcastic laugh.

"If I were not a gentleman and actually a savage like you say, you would have screamed so violently that the very walls of the library would have shaken, resonating your complete agony. Your mind would have fled, and you would have cried out to God, pleading with every fucking ounce of your being for Him to end this insufferable torment until the moment I would have shut you up forever myself."

I laugh hysterically. "You REALLY think you're a gentleman? How can you be so delusional?"

I sense his hand sliding out the magazine cautiously and press it against my chest.

"If I can make you drench a newsmag in so much cum, I allow myself, without shame, to take the title of gentleman."

He lets the wet object drop, its soft, damp thud against the cold blackand-white floor sounding louder than it should. He walks away, but after a few steps, he stops, glancing back with a vicious smile.

"And that," he says with mockery, "would make you the brat, little fox."

Chapter 7

XAN

*T*ucked away in a shadowed corner of the quiet street, I take a slow drag from my cigarette, letting the smoke travel in my lungs before flicking the butt into a storm drain. The glow dies instantly, swallowed by the undercity below.

Mira should step out any second now, heading off to work, completely unaware that the moment she locks her door behind her, I will be slipping inside. I have a gift for her, and I have spent enough time watching her to know her patterns, her habits.

The door to her apartment closes softly behind me and I stop for a moment, taking in the space's calmness. I notice the pristine order of her surroundings, every object carefully placed. Not a hint of personality, no signs of who she really is, just what he would approve of, I'm guessing.

She has her tiny painting room, and that is it. If she were mine, I would give her a goddamn manor—let her occupy every inch with whatever she wants.

I cross the corridor that leads to her bedroom, where the untouched bed stands, a quiet reminder of just how long it has been since it has seen any proper use. I cannot fucking wait to change that—to have her beneath me, rolling her eyes until she screams my name for all the neighbors to know what a little whore she is. To fill this room with my scent, my presence, my cum. A mark that will leave no doubt—Mira belongs with me.

Beyond the fact that I am going to give her the best damn orgasm she ever had in that bed, I stand here for a specific reason. I learned about a masquerade charity event days ago, piecing it together from snippets of conversation.

It was not difficult—Julian's name has a way of surfacing when she talks about her plans. She will be on his arm tonight, smiling for the cameras, playing the part of the perfect girlfriend. I know I can't stop her from going. But I can make sure she wears exactly what I want her to.

That is why I am here, to place carefully the red dress I selected that will command every eye in the room. A piece of fabric that, draped over Mira's voluptuous body, will possess the power to mesmerize even the most hardened of hearts. A daring slit climbs high up her thigh, the satin slipping like liquid over the curve of her hips, pooling at the floor.

And the neckline—bold, daring, and exquisitely cut—showcasing the undeniable allure of her generous breast. The dress of all dresses, the one I have meticulously chosen to leave an impression on everyone who dares to look—a silent command disguised as a gift.

For the mask, I could not get past the opportunity to give her the sumptuous appearance of the innocent animal she always reminds me of with her magnificent hair.

A fox—*my* little fox.

As I turn to leave, a notification pops on my phone to tell me she just sent a text to someone. I can feel my pulse quicken as I swipe open the message and realize it is meant for Julian, telling him how eager she is about the charity event. Her words are so kind, almost like she needs to prove herself. I cannot shake the image of her and Julian together. Her smile, his touch. The way she looked at him before... It felt genuine. And it drives me fucking crazy.

A grin creeps up on my face. By now, it is clear my interests are becoming anything but professional. I try to hold back, to suppress the rage rising inside me, still all I can think about is tearing his eyes out of their sockets for ever daring to lay them on my little fox.

She is mine, and I have never been known to share.

A quick glance at a picture of them together on her nightstand is the breaking point of my control. My fist slams into the frame, sending it crashing against the wall, shattering the glass as if it were my own restraint.

"YOU. DO. NOT. DESERVE HER!", I scream uncontrollably. My hand trembles, the force of my actions hitting me in the aftermath. The fury surges through me as I stare at the broken remnants of the frame on the floor.

What the hell was that?

This is not who I am. I absolutely fucking hate what she is doing to me, but I cannot stop it. For the first time in my life, my desires are entirely mine, and I won't let them slip through my fingers. The inferno inside me is way too strong to ignore, and it is too late to fight it now.

I take a step back, surveying the wreckage of my temper. The shattered frame lies in ruin on the floor, its glass shards reflecting the light. Julian's face—ripped, cracked beneath my boot.

It should be enough. It should be. But it is not.

The only pristine thing left on this side of the room is the dress. Bloodred silk draped over her bed, untouched by the violence surrounding it. It is waiting patiently for the right person to unleash the full extent of its power.

Just like her.

I run a hand through my hair, inhaling deeply, forcing me to settle just enough to make my exit. I can still hear my own ragged breath as I walk back through the apartment, each step measured, controlled—despite the chaos in my head.

My fingers brush the door handle as I pause.

What if she doesn't wear it? What if she looks at it and refuses to put it on? I picture her slipping into something else, something plain and dull, something *he* picked for her.

The thought burns through me.

Be patient.

She will wear it.

She will wear it because *I* chose it. Because *I* carved this moment into her life with my own hands.

Because, in the end, she's mine.

Chapter 8

MIRA

After a busy morning, I return home around noon with Julian to get ready for the gala tonight. I'm looking forward to the event, but more than anything, I just want a moment to breathe before the busy evening unfolds.

I set my bag down and shrug off my coat, already anticipating the routine ahead—shower, makeup, dress. Julian walks past me, stretching his arms as he heads toward the kitchen.

"It will be a long night, but at least there will be good champagne," he muses. "You should try to enjoy yourself a little."

He flashes me a half-smile before heading toward the bedroom. I hesitate before following. My mind is still tangled in the events of yesterday.

The library.

The dark corner where he had me pinned, his breath against my ear, his fingers trailing fire along my skin. His words had been a trap; one I had unconsciously stepped right into.

I can still feel the heat from that magazine pulsing inside me, the warmth flooding between my thighs. My breath quickens, just from the memory of the slow, firm pressure as his hands mapped every curve of my body, the ache, the rawness of it all.

"Damn, Mira."

Julian's voice snaps me back. He is standing by the bed, staring at something. My stomach drops.

"That's the dress you picked?"

He steps closer, eyes roaming over the deep red silk draped across my bed. He exhales sharply.

"Holy shit, babe. You're going to drive me insane wearing this."

I swallow hard, my pulse hammering in my ears. I did not pick that dress and even less the mask. But I know who did. I suddenly feel lightheaded, my fingers curling into my palms as I struggle to keep my expression neutral.

Julian lets out a low whistle, shaking his head.

"I won't be able to keep my hands off you tonight with this." He steps closer, tracing the fabric with his fingertips.

"I swear, you're trying to kill me. And if I get jealous? That's on you foxy."

I smile, nodding, pretending everything is fine. Yet my heart is trying to jump out of my chest. At least Julian doesn't notice the broken glass on the floor nor the shattered frame with the photo of us now fractured into sharp little pieces.

It is not random, and I know it.

I inspect the dress as Julian steps out of the bedroom to take a shower. It is sumptuous—elegant, seductive—everything I secretly love, but would never dare to wear. Paired with dark red lipstick and my fiery hair, it will be perfect.

But how does he know that? How does a man whose name I do not even recall understand me better than I understand myself? More importantly—what the hell did I do to attract a stalker in the first place?

I am the definition of unremarkable. I read, drink decaf coffee, occasionally go out with my best friend, and have an innocent obsession with orcas. Nothing about me screams *target*.

Without a second thought, I grab my phone, determined to get something out of him.

> Since you already burned an X into my arm like a fucking psychopath, the least you could do is tell me the rest of the letters.

I wait anxiously while looking at the screen, eager to read the answer.

I'll tell you when you'll be forced to scream it.

I don't know what I expected, but it sure wasn't this. The audacity, the cockiness radiating from him is beyond anything I could have imagined. It sets my blood boiling so intensely I can barely contain it.

Oh, I'll wear your dress, alright. But tonight, it's Julian who'll have me—while you watch from afar, helpless. He will be the one to touch me, to claim me in it, and you will be left to stew in your jealousy with only your sad dick to keep you company, unable to do a damn thing about it. 🖐

Proud and satisfied with my sharp retort, I toss my phone onto the bed, my pulse racing with anticipation. The moment I hear vibrating again, I spring toward it, a surge of adrenaline flooding through me. I need to see if it had the effect I craved, if my words landed as I intended, lighting whatever spark of frustration I was hoping for.

We'll see about that.

The words hang in the air like a challenge.

We'll see about that.

He cannot possibly confront Julian in front of all these people...

I'll be safe, I reassure myself. I will be shielded by my man, I know I'll be untouchable—protected, even if it is just for the night.

———— 𝒕 ————

A limousine pulls up in front of us. I clutch the satin of my dress, careful with each step as I descend the stairs—these black stiletto heels are treacherous, after all. Julian beams beside me, eager to parade me around.

He loves bringing me to these events, knowing I am the kind of woman who draws people in effortlessly. I know how to converse, how to smile at the right moment, how to carry myself with grace—the perfect companion.

I have always taken it as a compliment, the way he proudly shows me off on his arm. Tonight though, something feels off. Tonight, it does not feel like admiration, more like possession. For the first time, I wonder if I have been blind to it all along.

We have about thirty minutes ahead of us. I watch the city blur past the window, trying to steady my breath as the anticipation of the evening creepily settles over me. Julian's hand lands on my exposed thigh, his fingers pressing gently into my skin. A shiver coils beneath my skin—neither pleasure nor fear, just instinct. Automatic.

There is no denying he looks good. The navy suit, perfectly tailored. The crisp white shirt, undone just enough. He is handsome, undeniably so—masculine, refined, flawlessly put together. He smells expensive, clean, familiar.

And yet... his touch does nothing to me.

I try to convince myself that the recent event is to blame—that what happened left me unsettled, not in the right state of mind for intimacy. Deep down, I know that's not the truth, because I was not ready yesterday either.

None of it was asked for. None of it was voluntary. So why is it that the mere memory of his hand tightening around my throat sends a pulse of heat between my legs, while the touch of the man who I love—who should be the only one to affect me—feels like absolutely nothing at all?

Julian turns his head, his eyes locking onto me with undeniable hunger. I anticipated this moment the second I realized the gala was a full half-hour drive from the apartment. It is not right—how the simple expectation of being alone with the man who is supposed to be my other half fills me with more dread than excitement.

He runs his fingers through my hair, his voice dripping with sweetness as he murmurs how beautiful I am, how much he misses me. And I miss him too—or at least, I wish I did. More than anything, I miss myself. The version of me that did not feel like she was suffocating in moments like this.

He hands me a shot of vodka from the minibar, and I grasp it, downing it in one gulp.

"Another."

Julian smirks, that playful glint in his eyes tinged with something more—hope. He knows the only way I have been able to get close to him lately is with enough alcohol in my system to drown out the hesitation. So, he pours me another. Then a third. The air between us starts to feel lighter, the weight of his gaze less excruciating.

"You know, we've got just enough time for a little treat... Come on baby, it's been so long."

With a deliberate motion, he unbuckles his belt and drags down his zipper, the tension in his pants finally easing as he exposes exactly what he expects—what he demands—from me.

My phone vibrates, a sharp jolt against my leg. I steal a quick glance—just enough to catch the message.

Don't you dare.

What? But how?

Panic grips me as my eyes dart frantically around the limousine. It is simply impossible—there is no way he could know what I am doing right now. Unless... Maybe it is just a coincidence. A mind game. A bluff.

Fine. Let's find out.

Without breaking eye contact with Julian, I slide my hand over the hard length straining against his pants and begin to stroke, testing fate itself. His head falls back as a deep, satisfied groan escapes his lips.

Ironically, there is no unease—none of the usual discomfort that creeps in the shadows of our intimacy. Instead, a fierce determination takes hold of me, a competitive fire that refuses to be extinguished.

Oh, so you think you're watching me? You want me to believe that? Watch this.

Straightaway, I take him as far as I can, blowing his cock with overflowing energy.

"Fuck, babe—what the hell? That feels so fucking good. Don't stop. Like ever."

I don't plan to. Not until my phone vibrates again. Not until he begs me to.

I devour him with desperate hunger, my tongue tracing every inch as if I have been starving for days—as if tomorrow is the end of the world and this is my last chance to taste anything at all.

I realize that my arousal nearly rivals what I felt in the library. Forgotten sensations surge, igniting a compulsion that refuses to be tamed. I need more. I need *him* to answer me. I know that is what will push my desire past the point of no return. I crave the danger, to chase the adrenaline until it makes me tremble, driving me to the orgasm—until I shatter from the sheer thrill of it.

Just the memory of yesterday is enough to send my hand slipping between my legs, impatient to quell the unbearable ache surging. I almost never wear underwear, allowing my fingers to claim me as effortlessly as a blade sinking into silk—merciless, inevitable, and utterly intoxicating.

The deeper I suck him, the more desperate my fingers become, chasing a pleasure that borders on madness. His touch, once teasing, turns brutal—pulling my hair in a ruthless fist, forcing my head down despite the strain, despite the resistance that is more instinct than intent. My throat clenches tighter, my lungs beg for air, but the only sound that escapes is a muffled, sinful gasp.

Yet... still no message.

I realize I should drown in panic, but strangely I am not. A different kind of power coils, dark and insidious. Why am I pretending to resist when my whole being wants this?

I yield, leaning into the force of his hand, letting him drive me down as my own fingers mirror the motion, lost in the audacious, breathless thrill of surrender.

As the limousine shielding our depravity glides silently over the asphalt, a sudden burst of light flares ahead, followed by the raw growl of an engine.

"What the hell?" Julian snaps, straightening his suit as he leans angrily forward to get a better look through the window.

I follow his lead. A jolt shoots through me as soon as I see it—a motorcycle, sleek and black, parked sideways in the middle of the road, blocking our way. The rider sits motionless, dressed in all black, his face hidden beneath a helmet. Julian growls in frustration, shoving the door open.

"I swear to God—"

I barely register his anger as I step out behind him, my eyes locked onto the rider's back. He is completely still, like he's waiting for something—or someone. The limo's headlights cast long shadows, illuminating the sharp lines of his leather jacket, the stiffness in his shoulders.

For a moment, everything stands down—the city noise fading, Julian's frustrated muttering nothing but background static. My entire world narrows on the figure astride the bike, his broad shoulders tense, his head tilting ever so slightly as if considering whether to stay or go. He is a statue, frozen in time, yet I can feel his dominance piercing through the visor.

That's when I notice it.

A small screen mounted on the side of his bike, glowing in the darkness. On it—clear as day—is the inside of the limousine. Every corner of it. Every moment.

Nausea rises in my throat.

It is him. He *was* watching me.

I take a step forward, but before I can say anything, he's gone. The motorcycle speeds off into the night, leaving only the echo of its engine and the icy realization sinking into my bones.

By the time we finally pull up to the gala, I am practically clawing at the door to get out. The air inside the limo feels suffocating, thick with Julian's petulant silence.

He spent the entire drive brooding, furious that I did not finish what he so desperately wanted. As if that were my fault.

As if I could have possibly ignored the way my entire body locked up the second *he* appeared.

The event is held at a mansion so extravagant it looks like something out of a Hollywood fever dream. Towering white columns stretch toward the night sky, framing an entrance flanked by golden fountains that shimmer under soft, ambient lighting. Flowers spill from massive, ornate pots, their fragrance mixing with the crisp evening air. It is a scene designed to impress, to dazzle. Inside, the opulence only intensifies.

The moment we step through the doors, a server appears with a tray of champagne. I snatch a glass and swallow it in one go, the chilled bubbled liquid burning as it rushes down my throat.

The server's lips press into a disapproving line, her eyes hovering just a second too long. Like I care. Try sitting in a car while your boyfriend sulks like a child because your stalker nearly caused a crash just to stop him from finishing getting blown. You would chug your drink too, sweetheart.

I take the time to secure my mask, adjusting it until it fits just right. I have to admit, I finally understand the allure—the sense of anonymity, the quiet power it brings. It feels like an armor, a barrier shielding me from wandering eyes and hidden intentions. There is something peculiar about it, something that makes me stand taller.

I glance at Julian beside me, with a gleaming white half-mask, reminiscent of the Phantom of the Opera. The scowl he has been wearing since we arrived disappears the second a distinguished man approaches—a top executive from the company Julian has been bending over backward to impress.

"Ah, Mr. Miller! Your home is absolutely gorgeous!" Julian exclaims, slipping effortlessly into charming mode.

The man's smile is practiced, polite. When his attention lands on me, a flicker of intrigue appears. He takes my hand, bringing it to his lips with ease.

"Not nearly as gorgeous as your wife, Julian. Now, this—" his eyes sweep over me, staring just long enough to make my skin prickle—"this is a true work of art, Beckett."

Heat floods my face, my blush no doubt rivaling the deep crimson of my dress. I force a gracious smile, my voice steady despite the constricting pressure in my chest.

"Thank you for the invitation, Mr. Miller. Your home is truly remarkable."

He still hasn't let go of my hand. Instead, he strengthens his hold, keeping me close.

"For you, my dear, it's Simon. And had I known a vision like you existed, I would have extended an invitation much, much sooner."

With a slow, purposeful wink, he presses one last persistent kiss to my hand before finally releasing me. Julian does not seem the least bit fazed, as if this kind of exchange is nothing out of the ordinary. Honestly, I'm not surprised. Sometimes, I get the unsettling feeling that if offering me up could secure his coveted position, he would not hesitate.

I know I am being dramatic—but then again, am I?

Before I can dwell on it, two more men join our little circle. One of them has a woman on his arm, a girl so young the age gap alone could make heads turn in outrage. She leans in, her perfume sickly sweet, her lips barely moving as she whispers in my ear.

"I'd start drinking if I were you."

Her words brush against me, leaving a faint chill in their wake. I turn slightly, catching the wary glint in her eyes before she hides it with a fake smile.

What is that supposed to mean?

I do not get the chance to ask. The men launch into a conversation about market trends and investment strategies— one I have absolutely no interest in—but the woman beside me doesn't move away. She keeps her glass close to her mouth, and I notice she barely drinks.

Julian, oblivious or simply indifferent, is already deep in discussion with Simon and the others, nodding along and laughing. Meanwhile, the girl turns her head slightly, her focus flickering between them before settling back on me.

"You're new to these, aren't you?" she murmurs, her tone laced with something I can't quite place. Amusement? Pity, maybe?

I straighten my shoulders, unwilling to let her see any hint of hesitation.

"No," I lie smoothly. "...Why?"

She exhales a soft chuckle, swirling the champagne in her glass.

"No reason," she says, but there is something knowing in her smirk. She leans in again, her voice lower this time. "Just... don't let them get you alone."

A shiver dances down my spine. I force out a laugh, pretending I did not hear the warning beneath her words, but I can feel my fingers clawing around the stem of my glass.

She shrugs. "You'll see soon enough."

With that, she turns away, slipping seamlessly back into the role of the perfect, lovely companion. But I cannot shake the tension settling in my stomach.

What the hell did I just walk into?

Chapter 9

XAN

Mira does not belong in this world.

The only place she belongs is with me, by my side, in my arms. Not in this sea of polished sharks, dressed in their finest suits, flashing their power and wealth like warning signs with price tags. I should tear their eyes out for daring to lay them on her, but damn, I cannot deny it— she wears it better than anyone ever could.

The deep red of her dress clings to her like skin, the slit teasing glimpses of smooth skin with every step she takes. Her hair is a cascade of fire, a stark contrast to the fox mask that hides just enough of her face to make me want to rip it off. To remind her she cannot hide from me, because I do not want her to. She will have to learn that I am here for her own good, that she needs me to survive.

An unexpected message shatters the trance my girl's body had cast over me.

> If you don't give me something useful tonight,
> I will handle this myself.

I exhale slowly, forcing my grip to loosen.

Handle this himself?

That could mean anything. A threat. A warning. A reminder of who's really in charge. In any way, I cannot let that happen.

Mira stands near the dance floor, ignorant of the importance of the words on my screen. I force myself to look away from her and scan the room. First, I must deal with the men.

They stand in a loose circle, expensive whiskey in hand, talking like they own everything. One of them—older, well-dressed, the type that takes without asking—tilts his glass toward Mira.

"She is something, isn't she?" he muses, eyes trailing over her.

I take a sip of my drink, even though the impulse to slit his throat right here, right now, is intensely strong, I stay silent.

"She keeps looking at me," he continues. "Waiting for a real man to come claim her properly."

Fucking liar.

"She doesn't seem like the type to say yes easily," another man comments.

The older one chuckles.

"They never do. Well, not at first at least."

I let out a low laugh, shaking my head as if amused.

"You just need the right setting," I say smoothly as I approach the group. "Somewhere quieter. Somewhere she can't make a scene."

His lips curl into a pleased smirk.

Good. Take the bait.

Because the moment he gets her alone, I am going to be there. I will make sure he never looks at her again.

"I think I'll give it a go. Gentlemen."

I finish my sentence with a playful wink, making my new 'friends' laugh, egging me on. They are such disgusting pieces of shit. They deserve to have one of them gutted, and another strung up by with his intestines.

Of course, I smother the impulse. I need to find a way to speak to Mira, to get through to her without her running off in terror.

Instead of walking towards her direction, I head for Julian, puffing up his chest in front of his colleagues, telling some idiotic story about how women are like stocks. They can rise in value, but one wrong move, and they are worthless.

"That is why you've got to keep them well-maintained," I interrupt. "They are just like cars. You put money into them and then you're ready to take them for a ride."

Julian laughs heartily, extending his hand toward me, free from his champagne flute.

"A man with such wisdom, please—tell me your name!"

At that exact moment, Mira's eyes meet mine. The strain in her look, the hardening of her lips, tells me everything I need to know—she knows.

She recognizes my black leather mask.

I take Julian's hand with a fierce, unwavering hold, never breaking my stare with her.

"Hayes. My name is Xan Hayes."

Chapter 10

MIRA

The audacity of this man—whose identity is no longer a mystery—knows no bounds. How dare he walk up to us, insert himself even further into my life, as if he had not already invaded every part?

He challenges Julian, that much is obvious. But more than that, he reminds me—shows me—that he is in control of the situation. Even here, in a place that does not belong to him, he owns the moment.

"Would I be so fortunate as to steal your enchanting creature for a dance?" he asks, his tone dripping with something mischievous and amused.

I seize Julian's arm firmly.

"No, thank you. My boyfriend doesn't like to share."

Xan drags a hand through his tousled hair, laughter rolling off him with infuriating ease.

"If I had you at my side, I wouldn't like to share either," he says, each word measured. "In fact, I wouldn't ever share at all. I would keep you to myself—forever. Just to make sure no one else could ever lay claim to what should only be mine."

I laugh. "Wow, that sounded exactly like something a guy with women locked in his basement would say."

I catch the subtle narrowing of his eyes.

"I might. What is it to you? Want a room?"

I turn to Julian, expecting him to intervene, to put an end to whatever this is. But he says nothing. He looks everywhere but at me.

"You know what?" I hear myself say, my voice steadier than I feel. "I accept."

Xan darkens behind his mask. He steps in, so close I can feel the heat of him as he murmurs just for me—

"Good girl."

The moment his hand clasps mine, a bolt of electricity surges, flooding my veins, sharp and instant, just as the first languid notes of *Earned It* by *The Weeknd* pulse through the air. He is unshaken, grounding me, as if I belong there—no, as if I *must* be there with him. He pulls my arm onto the dance floor with a charismatic drawl, his gaze never wavering, never releasing me.

I have, at any point, felt like the only person in a room before. Not like this. Everything around me blurs, the world slipping into slow motion. The music drowns out all other noises, weaving around my senses, intoxicating me. The moment I step into the spotlight at the center of the floor, I feel their eyes—hundred of strangers subtly watching, glancing, whispering.

I am seen. I am alive.

Xan tugs my hand, and in one swift, commanding movement, I crash against his body, our forms molding together as though we were always meant to be one. His hand glides down the curve of my spine, igniting a trail of heat in its wake.

Just as it nears the edge of something forbidden, he stops—hovering, teasing, testing the limits of restraint. The unbearable anticipation coils in my core, leaving me breathless with the unspoken promise lingering between us.

It is almost surreal, watching him move like this, understanding now what had seemed impossible in the library's event. He had told me he was a gentleman, and I had scoffed at the absurdity of the statement. But here, beneath the dim glow of chandeliers and the burn of his presence, I understand the gravity of his words.

A rogue strand of hair falls against my cheek. He brushes it back and leans in, his voice a murmur against my skin.

"Can't you see how beautiful you are, Mira?" His breath is warm, honeyed, dangerous. "Every look in this room is on you. The women, envious. The men, hungry."

A flicker of panic sparks in my chest. I look around—he is right. They are watching. Their stares are sharp, dissecting. I tense. My body reacts before my mind does, trying to pull away.

Xan won't allow it.

His grip tightens—not harsh, but unyielding, as if he is anchoring me, as if he knows I am teetering on the precipice of something vast and consuming. He leans in closer, his cheek brushing mine, his scent wrapping around me like smoke.

"But you know what, little fox?" His voice is softer now, more treacherous in its restraint. "You may not be on my arm tonight, not officially. However, it is clear to everyone in this room right now—you *belong* to me."

A breath leaves me, something between surrender and relief. For a fleeting, impossible moment, I exist. Not as a ghost, not as a muted version of myself, but as something vivid, something real. My head feels heavy, my body light, and I fight the urge to rest against the shoulder of his impeccably tailored black suit.

I am hypnotized. Like a serpent lulled into submission by a song only it can hear, I listen. I obey. I yield.

And I hate it. I should hate it. I *have* to hate it.

But I don't.

I don't, because euphoria has already slithered its way into my veins, curling into a dark, primal force.

That is when I see Julian.

Standing at the threshold of the dance floor, his posture stiff, his hands clenched into fists. His frustration ripples through the space, barely contained.

Of course, *now* he notices me. Now, when another man has stripped me bare without ever touching my skin. Now, when someone else has awakened something in me he never could.

Xan sees it too. He starts laughing—low, quiet, predatory.

"That's it," he whispers, watching my eyes focused on Julian's growing anger. "Show him who you really are, Mira. Show him what he is losing—what he will never have again."

His fingers press just slightly at my waist, enough to make my pulse stutter.

"Because I won't let you dance with another man... Ever"

A pause. A promise.

"You belong to me on this dance floor," he breathes. "And for the rest of our lives."

As the song fades into silence, the burden of the world crashes down on my shoulders once more. Xan takes my hand, and for a fleeting second, I think he might hold onto it. Instead, he turns, giving it back to Julian. The warmth of his skin vanishes, leaving behind nothing but a hollow ache.

"You should keep her on a leash before one of these men kidnaps her just for himself," Xan sneers, slipping back into the arrogant, cruel persona he wore so effortlessly earlier.

Julian chuckles, shaking his head.

"She is gorgeous, I'll give you that. But the second they'll try living with her, they'll let her go soon enough."

Xan muscles constrict, the vein in his neck throbbing. His hands clench at his sides, his jaw locked. He wants to hit him. I can see it. Feel it. Still, he restrains himself, forcing the fire in his veins to smolder instead of erupting.

With a deep breath, he turns away—walking back toward the bar with an air of careless ease, as if none of it ever mattered. As if he doesn't still crave the feel of me under his hands. I should be relieved that this is over, that I am free from whatever spell I had fallen under. But it does not come as freedom. Just the heavy ache of grief—like something precious has been ripped from me, and I have no choice but to let it go.

Julian's arm snakes around my waist, pulling me toward him.

"Come," he says, already lost in his own thoughts. "One of the senior partners wants to talk to me upstairs. This is it." His voice is brimming with anticipation. "I'm finally getting the offer of being a partner. The others all said they went through the same thing before their promotion. You will wait in a lounge outside his office. Someone will keep you company."

The girl's warning echoes in my mind.

Don't let them get you alone.

Every instinct screams at me to refuse, to make up some excuse, but Julian's grasp intensifies, daring me to resist. So I climb the stairs, dread curling around my ribs with each step. I barely hear the music anymore; my ears filled with the pounding of my heart. The walls are lined with portraits of men—generations of power and wealth immortalized in gold frames. Their eyes seem to follow me, judging, knowing something that I don't.

At the top of the staircase, a man greets Julian like an old friend. His boss, I assume. He barely acknowledges me before dragging him away into an adjacent office. I exhale shakily; my nerves frayed and sink into one of the opulent green velvet sofas in the room I waited.

The lounge is extravagant, its decor meant to intimidate, to remind you of your place. The music is still in the background, muffled, but persistent. I close my eyes, trying to breathe through the anxiety brewing in my stomach.

Without notice—icy fingers, firm and possessive, press my exposed thigh. I jolt, a small gasp slipping past my lips.

"Easy now, honey. It's just me."

The voice is smooth, a bit familiar. I open my eyes to see the same man Julian had been speaking to earlier, the one who had watched me just a little too closely. I force a weak smile, hoping—*praying*—that he is just drunk, that this is some terrible misunderstanding. But as I move to stand, his hand slides higher. Before I can react, he grabs my breast, fingers digging in without shame.

"Alright," I say, forcing steadiness. "Clearly, you've had too much champagne. Let me go, or my boyfriend is going to handle this for me."

He laughs. Low, condescending. Like I just said the most amusing thing in the world.

"Julian?" He smirks. "Sweetheart, he would sell his own mother for this promotion. *You?* You were just part of the deal!"

Everything stops. I cannot breathe. I cannot think. The world crashes violently as his words settle deep into my bones, poisoning everything I thought I knew. Julian would not...

I try to move, to fight, but my limbs feel heavy, useless. My mind fragments, detaching from my body as his hands continue their invasion. I feel everything and nothing all at once.

I am slipping. Fading. My legs give out beneath me. I am falling. And just as I realize it—just as the darkness swallows me whole—it is already too late.

Chapter 11

XAN

The plan was simple.

Slip into the gala unnoticed, track Mira, and extract whatever information Lucian needed.

What actually happened?

Julian now knows my real name. I've made an absolute spectacle of myself by pulling her into a dance that bordered on a public declaration of possession. And worst of all—I lost her.

My eyes scan the ballroom, sweeping over the sea of masks and expensive suits. She's gone. *They're gone.* A sickening, ice-cold certainty creeps through my veins. Nothing good can come of this. If one of those bastards has laid a single, filthy hand on her, I swear—I will carve him open from sternum to spine and string his insides across this fucking mansion like Christmas lights.

I overheard Julian earlier. Whispering to Simon about a trade. About an offer. I know exactly where high-stakes deals are usually made.

The offices. Upstairs.

I slide my knife from its holster, tucking it into my sleeve, every nerve locked onto one single thought.

Find her. Now.

My instincts have never failed me—not once. They have kept me alive in the darkest pits of this world. And right now? They are screaming at me. Screaming that I need to move. That I need to save her.

I take the stairs two at a time. That's when I hear it. Mira's voice. Strained. Smothered beneath the guttural rasp of a man's laughter.

The moment I push open the door, my world narrows to a singular, bloodstained reality. She's on the ground, legs forced apart, the delicate fabric of her dress torn like it was never meant to be anything but a sacrifice.

He is on top of her. Pinning her down. Mira thrashes, her nails clawing at the asshole's face, but he is bigger. Stronger. Overpowering her. Unlike when I had her in my arms yesterday, her body is stiff, rigid with horror. She does not want this. She is absolutely terrified.

Rules lodge themself in my mind, many I have obeyed since childhood. *Do not interfere. Do not intervene. Stay detached.*

Follow the mission. But this? This has nothing to do with precision. Nothing to do with discipline. This is about her.

And the *only* person allowed to break her is *me.*

My knife glides into my palm. In a single, fluid motion, I bury it in his throat. The steel tears through flesh, slicing from one side to the other. Mira screams. The man gurgles, a wet, choking sound as his body convulses, blood surging from his throat in thick, crimson waves. It floods down, drenching her in warmth, mingling with the red of her dress until there is no distinction between fabric and death.

I grab a fistful of his hair before he can collapse on top of her. My blade slides free, and I turn my head toward Mira—only her.

She's staring at me. Not with fear. Not with horror. But something else. Something raw. Something I own. I lower my voice, quiet but seething, laced with darkness and absolute.

"This is my first gift to you."

"And I promise, little fox—there will be many more."

With merciless precision, I press my blade against the inner corner of his eye and push. He jerks, still barely alive, spasming as I work the knife deeper, until the socket gives way. Until his eyeball detaches. His remaining eye widens in sheer agony, and for a brief, glorious moment, I hold him there—force him to watch as I finish what I started.

The second the eye threatens to pop free, I yank the knife back, shove my fingers into the gaping wound, and rip it out myself. It dangles between my fingers, slick and warm, the optic nerve twitching like it still understands the magnitude of its suffering.

I lift it, just enough for him to see what I have done before the final breath rattles from his chest. I let his corpse slump forward, his dead weight hitting the ground with a dull thud.

I turn back to her, stepping closer, knife still slick with his blood, and tilt her chin up with the blade. My voice is a whisper, a vow, a death sentence to every man who will ever think of touching her again.

"This is for you, Mira."

"And it will happen again. And again. And *again*—to anyone who dares lay eyes on what belongs to me."

I glance down at the scumbag's corpse, his head lolling unnaturally, blood still pooling beneath him. The slash across his throat gapes wide, his eye socket an empty, oozing void. If I leave him like this, someone will definitely ask questions.

And I do not want questions. I want fear.

I kneel beside him, take his chin, and force his head back into position. His jaw flaps uselessly, slack and bloodied, but I do not need him to talk. I just need him to *speak*.

I retrieve my weapon, still warm from his flesh, and carve a mark across his cheek—curling a circled 'T' that the right people will recognize. A *signature*, unmistakable to those who operate in the shadows of this city.

The Obsidian Order does not tolerate weakness. They sure as hell don't tolerate their members being taken out like this. Whoever finds him will assume one thing—*he was punished*. And no one questions a punishment.

I lift the body by the shoulders and drag it toward the farthest end of the room. There is a small, round table, barely used. I prop him up in one of the high-backed chairs, straightening his posture, letting his head fall slightly forward as if he's simply slumped in thought. I fix his collar, wipe a smear of blood from his lips with my sleeve. From the outside, it looks almost... peaceful.

Almost.

The final touch? I take his missing eye—the one I ripped from his skull—and place it carefully in his palm, fingers curled around it like a gift. An offering. A *warning*. Anyone who walks in here will know exactly what this means.

I turn back to her, scanning the mess of her appearance. She looks wrecked. Not just by what happened, but by me. Her dress—ruined. Torn at the hem, stained a deep, damning crimson. Her hands, shaking, still slick with his blood. If she walks out like this, they will stop us.

I unbutton my tuxedo jacket and drape it over her shoulders, shielding as much of her body as I can. However, the fabric won't hide the way she moves—the stiffness, the shock.

Think, Hayes. Think.

The coat check.

There is a hallway nearby—one meant for staff, yet open to guests who know where to look. I grab her wrist, tugging her toward it, ignoring how cold she feels beneath my touch.

We reach a storage closet. I yank the door open, searching through shelves of coats, scarves, anything. My fingers brush over something soft—cashmere. A long, elegant wrap, perfect for draping over her shoulders, over her shame.

"Lift your arms."

She obeys without question, letting me wrap the fabric around her like I am dressing a doll. Her hands are still bloody. I grab a champagne bucket from a nearby table, the ice half-melted, and thrust her hands into the freezing water. She gasps, but I don't let go. I rub her fingers together beneath the surface, watching the water darken, swirl.

"Stay still," I order. She does.

I dry her hands with a cloth napkin, then take her chin between my fingers, tilting her face toward mine. Inspecting her.

"If anyone asks, you spilled wine. You got sick. You're drunk. Whatever. Say anything else, and I will fucking drag you out of here kicking and screaming, *understood*?"

Her lips press together. She nods.

The front is too exposed. Too many eyes. Too many questions. Instead, I guide her through the service hallway, past waiters carrying trays of champagne and plates of caviar. No one stops us. Nobody even notices.

Outside, the crisp night air cuts through the stench of blood, replacing it with gasoline, smoke, the distant promise of rain. I pull Mira closer, pressing a hand to the small of her back.

A valet eyes us curiously. I flash a couple of crisp hundred-dollar bills, muttering, "*No questions.*"

He hands me a set of keys without a word. Seconds later, we are in a sleek black car, gliding away from the scene like shadows slipping through the cracks of a city that never really sleeps. She's staring out the window, unmoving, her face unreadable in the dim light.

Still processing.

I don't speak. Not yet.

Mira's silence presses against my chest, heavy and expectant. I keep my eyes on the road, but my focus drifts to her—the set of her shoulders, the tension in her jaw. She hasn't asked where we are going. Or why. She hasn't looked at me once.

I expect fear. Accusations. Maybe even disgust.

And I would not blame her.

She saw just enough to know something's wrong—with me, with all of this. And if she did not, she will soon. I have done things no apology could ever erase. If she knew the half of it, she would already be running.

So, I drive. And wait for the moment she finally breaks the mute atmosphere.

She has not moved much. Just sits there, staring out the window like the world outside might make more sense than the one she's in now. I glance at her once. Then again.
Still nothing. No questions. No screaming. Just silence, coiled and ready to snap.

I fucking hate this part. The waiting. The not knowing what version I'll get when it finally breaks.

I shift my grip on the wheel. Clear my throat. Think about saying something—but nothing useful comes to mind.

What the hell am I supposed to say anyway?

Then she turns. Slow. Mechanical.

Her eyes find mine.

"You killed him."

She finally speaks. Her voice is shaky. Mine isn't.

"No. I saved you."

Chapter 12

MIRA

The city lights blur past in streaks of gold and orange as Xan drives, his grip white-knuckled on the wheel. The speedometer creeps higher, but I barely feel the momentum. My body is frozen, locked in place, the blood drying on my skin like a second layer of flesh. It is not mine.

The scent of iron is strong, suffocating. My dress—once sleek and elegant—now clings to my body in wet patches, ruined. The fabric sticks to my thighs, my stomach, my chest. My hands shake, my breath comes in shallow bursts, still I cannot seem to move. To speak. To do anything but stare at the dark smudges of red staining my fingers that won't come off. I rub my palms against my thighs, desperate to make it disappear. But the more I scrub, the deeper it seems to sink in. The more real it becomes.

I can still hear it. The gurgling sound as the man bled out on top of me. The wet squelch of flesh being torn. The ragged gasps as Xan ripped his eye from its socket.

A sound escapes me—caught between a sob and a whimper. He refuses to look at me. Says nothing. Just drives.

The silence in the car is a noose, tightening around my throat with every second that passes. I know I should say something—anything—but what words could possibly fit?

How do you talk after witnessing that? After being a part of it? Because I was. I might not have held the knife, but I felt the life drained from that man's body. I felt it. And I never looked away.

What does that make me?

The tires screech as Xan takes a sharp turn, snapping me out of my thoughts. My body lurches sideways. The seatbelt digs into my chest, keeping me anchored.

He is driving recklessly, pushing the car to its limits, weaving through traffic with lethal ease. Obviously, he has done this before. Panic flutters weakly in my stomach.

"Where are we going..." My voice is hoarse, barely above a whisper.

He exhales sharply through his nose, fingers flexing around the wheel.

"Somewhere safe." I swallow.

"Safe from who?"

Finally, he glances at me. Just for a second. But it is enough. His eyes through his mask—cold, dark, unreadable—show no comfort. "No one yet," he says. "But that will change soon." I shudder.

The car speeds through the night, and I press my forehead against the cool glass, watching as the world blurs past.

I should be relieved that I made it out of there alive. That he got me out of there. Yet all I can think about is Julian. The way he looked at me when he led me up those stairs. Like he knew. Like he had already accepted the cost of what he had done. Did he knew what they were going to do to me? Or did he just not care?

I close my eyes, my belly churning. I loved him. I shared a life with him. And in the end, I was just another price he was willing to pay. The ugliness of the world rises in my chest, twisting, curling into something that doesn't feel like grief.

It's hate.

The car jerks to a stop, yanking me from my thoughts once again. I blink, disoriented. We are in front of an old, run-down building, the kind people don't ask questions about. The neon sign above the entrance flickers weakly, casting eerie shadows on the pavement. Xan kills the engine and turns to me.

"Inside. Now."

I hesitate, my pulse hammering.

He sighs, running a hand through his hair.

"Mira, don't make me carry you because I promise you, it will not be gentle."

The way he says my name—so casual, so familiar—makes my skin prickle. He gets out first, slamming the door shut before stalking around to my side. I scramble to unbuckle my seatbelt, fumbling with the latch as he wrenches my door open.

"Move."

I move. The second my feet hit the pavement, reality slams into me violently. My knees buckle. The ground rushes up to meet me, but before I can hit it, firm hands seize my arms, hauling me upright. Xan's face is inches from mine.

"You're in shock," he mutters.

I let out a shaky breath, my fingers curling into the front of his shirt without thinking. His body tenses. I should let go. But I don't. I can't. This is unraveling, I am breaking apart at the seams, and the only thing anchoring me to reality is *him*. The smell of leather and blood. The raw, undeniable strength he has inside of him. I trail my hand up his chest, feeling the rapid, thunderous beat of his heart beneath my fingertips.

As much as I wish otherwise, mine is just as out of control. The night itself is to blame, of course—but more than that, it is him. The searing heat of his body, the electric charge pulsing between us. He is intoxicating, overwhelming, and I don't know if I actually want to pull away. Maybe I could not even if I tried. The last shred of energy I have left is spent on keeping my gaze locked onto his.

Without thinking, I grab his hand and pin it against my chest, forcing him to feel the erratic pounding beneath my ribs. His breath hitches, and I feel the subtle shift in his muscles, the tension winding like a predator holding itself back. I press harder, refusing to let go, silently begging him to understand. I want more—I want his hands to move, to explore, to claim me in a way that leaves no room for doubt.

I want him to ruin me.

He remains still, a living fortress of self-control. Except his body betrays him. I feel his dick, hard against my thigh. A silent confession in his pants. He knows I know. A sensual, measured roll of my hips against him, a wordless promise that hunger is not one-sided.

Still, he doesn't move or react. Just clenches his jaw, as if forcing himself to withstand the pull between us. I reach for him, my hand sliding lower, needing to feel more—to take what I crave—but before I can, his fingers close brutally around my wrist.

"Do not start something you cannot finish, Mira."

The words slice through the dense atmosphere; a warning wrapped in steel. My head jerks up, offended.

"Excuse me? Who the fuck are you to decide what I can or cannot handle?"

Xan exhales sharply, clearly exasperated.

"What happened in the library? That was nothing. Just a taste. You are not ready for what I would do to you."

My fury ignites, white-hot and violent. I shove him, slapping his torso with a trembling hand.

"You don't know a damn thing about me! You think you do because you have stalked my every move, but you are sooo blind. You know what? I... I fucking hate you!"

He huffs out a laugh, dry and taunting.

"You are such a brat." His smirk is infuriating. "Now that I think about it, maybe I should have left you there. Let that bastard take you like a worthless little whore, then send you crawling back to your garbage boyfriend—the one who respects a prostitute more than his own woman."

My palm strikes his face before I even register moving. The crack echoes like a gunshot in the quiet.

"And you think you're better than him?" My voice is pure venom. "Hiding behind that mask like some untouchable fucking fever dream. *Oh*, look at me, I'm a big, scary killer. I'm dangerous. I'm so fucking mysterious." I sneer. "You know what you really are, Xan? A fucking coward!"

The second the words leave my mouth, I know I have pushed him too far. He growls, a deep, animalistic sound, before grabbing me in one swift, brutal motion.

"Baby, I'm your worst nightmare—and your best addiction."

In an instant, I am thrown over his shoulder like I weigh nothing.

"Put me down!" I scream, pounding my fists against his back. He does not even flinch. "You piece of shit! Let me go!"

No one comes. No one stops him. I keep thrashing, but it is useless. He carries me effortlessly through the door, stepping into an unfamiliar place. The air changes, sterile and cold. My stomach twists. The walls are a pristine lifeless white, illuminated by dim, soulless lights. Everything is precise, calculated. It is the kind of place that does not belong to a man.

It belongs to a monster.

It is the kind of home you find in a psychological thriller. The kind of setting that makes you realize you might not walk out alive. The IKEA '*I Have Severe Mental Issues*' collection. And I am trapped in it.

Xan leads me through a narrow hallway, past a door with a busted lock, into a room with a single bed, a chair, and the bare necessities for a bathroom in the corner.

"Shower," he orders, releasing me right on the floor.

I stay still. He rubs a hand down his mask, his patience fraying.

"Mira, get in that damn shower, or I swear I will throw you in myself. And trust me, I have no problem knocking you out to make it happen."

"Would that make you feel better?" My voice shakes. "Stripping me down again and washing your mess off of me?"

His expression darkens. "*My* mess?"

"Yes! *Yours*! I never asked for *this*—I certainly never asked for *you*!"

A silent strain settles in his posture, but he remains unmoved. I laugh at the edge of hysteria.

"You act like you saved me, but you just made me *yours* instead of *his*. This was your plan all along, was is not, you fucking psychopath?"

His hand wraps around my throat, slamming me against the wall with a force that steals the breath from my lungs. My vision flickers, my pulse hammering beneath his grip. He leans in, his lips behind his mask grazing my ear as his voice drops to a dark, taunting whisper.

"If you think you are struggling to breathe now, just wait until my cock is buried so deep in your throat you forget what air even tastes like."

I swallow, my mouth constricting as my vision blurs, my eyes filling with unshed tears. His hands on my neck are without mercy, fingers pressing harshly to remind me who is in control. His voice is low, a slowburning threat wrapped in velvet.

"I'm going to let you go," he murmurs as I feel the heat of his breath ghost over my skin. "And you have until the count of three to strip and get in that fucking shower. If you hesitate, I will make you. Understand?" My stomach clenches. I nod, barely able to breathe.

"One."

My hands fumble as I turn away from him, my pulse hammering in my ears. I grasp the fabric of my dress, peeling it away with trembling fingers, the weight of his stare burning into my back.

"Two."

Humiliation inhabits me like a vice, still I force myself to keep moving. The dress slides down my body, pooling at my feet, exposing bare skin to the cool air. My lungs seize mid-inhale as I lift a leg to step into the shower, but suddenly—I freeze.

Am I really doing this? Stripping at the command of a man who has total control over me. Have I really fallen this far? Letting him dictate my every move, disintegrating every ounce of self-respect I once had?

"Tic, tac. Three."

Before I can react, a fist tangles in my hair, yanking me backward with a cruel pull. A choked gasp rips from my throat as I stumble, collapsing onto my knees. The marble floor is cold against my skin, my muscles locked in place, every ounce of defiance drained from my limbs. His hand cinches more roughly, twisting the strands of my hair between his fingers. A leash—an unbreakable one.

"You think you have choices, little fox?" he breathes, tone dripping with amusement. "Well, you don't. Not with me."

Heat floods my veins—anger, fear, darkness crawling inside me. Hating him would be easier. Cleaner. However, the way he restrains me completely, the way he dominates every inch of space between us, makes it impossible to ignore the way my body betrays me.

"Unzip."

I hesitate, my fingers trembling. His hand constricts enough to make my scalp prickle with pain. He lowers his voice to a near growl.

"I said—*unzip.*"

Tears spill over as I obey. With shaky movements, I reach up and pull the zipper down. The sound is deafening in the room's silence. The growing bulge strains against his pants, pressing insistently against the fabric, demanding release. Only his boxers still stand as a barrier. I know it won't be for long, the command should follow soon.

It's messed up—this whole thing is. And yet, I'm not repulsed. Not even close.

Is my life has spiraled into something so pathetic, so meaningless, that all I crave is to feel wanted? To feel like I still serve a purpose—to someone, to anything.

Right now, I realize how utterly futile my existence has become. If I disappeared forever, who would truly miss me? Zoey, of course. But after that? A father who died when I was seven, nothing but a vague memory wrapped in childhood amnesia. PTSD, they call it. And a mother who always preferred the bottle over me. I have nothing left.

I *had* Julian—yes, *had.* But did I ever really have him? How long had he been planning this betrayal? How many moments were lies? The questions exhaust me. Everything exhausts me.

"I don't know what is going through your head right now," Xan whispers. "But I need you to stay with me. Just for a moment. I *need* this, Mira."

His words should not affect me the way they do, but something about the way he says my name—almost pleading—unsettles me more than any threat ever could.

His free hand moves unexpectedly, fingers brushing my cheek, catching a tear before it falls. The contrast is dizzying, the tenderness of the gesture at complete odds with the way he still tugs at my hair.

Every instinct says to push him away, to fight the second I can. Regardless, I find myself frozen, trapped somewhere between fear and something I refuse to name. My pulse hammers against my ribs as I stare up at him, searching for a trace of the man who wiped my tears only moments ago.

His hold is steady—not harsh, but inescapable. His free hand moves calmly, trailing up my arm, brushing over my skin.

"Say something."

I can't.

His fingers tangle deeper in my hair—not in a violent tug, just enough to make me jump. His patience is thinning; I can feel it in the way his muscles coil, in the sharp exhale through his nose.

Still, as if the feeling in him shifts, he releases me just enough to let me do it from free will.

A test. I know it. And I hate that some pieces of me want to pass. I lift a trembling hand, hesitating before it lands on his chest. His heartbeat is a steady, heavy drum beneath my fingertips, matching the erratic rhythm of my own.

He watches me, waiting, when I finally whisper, "I don't know if I can do this..."

Envy flickers in his eyes and instead of pressing, demanding, he leans in.

"Then let me help you."

It would be a lie to say I don't ache for him—his body, his cock. The sheer proximity of him is utterly magnetic, and I want to taste every inch of him.

Without releasing my hair, he finally frees his eager length with his other hand. My eyes widen at the sight of it—thick, hard, imposing. A perfect match for the rest of him, every part sculpted and proportional, a masterpiece of raw masculinity. The swollen tip barely grazes my lips, sending a shiver down my spine.

"Open wide for me, Mira."

Unlike earlier, there is no hesitation. I want this. The perfect escape from the wreckage my life has become.

This is my time. This is survival.

My mouth parts as I let the tip drag against it, the heat of his skin igniting fire deep inside me. My tongue flicks over the head, savoring his taste. Before I can take control, he yanks my neck back. I resist, reclaiming my movement as I take him deeper, more than half of his length disappearing into my mouth in one languid, eager stroke.

"Damn, Mira... your mouth was fucking made for me. This is pure perfection."

His words send a sharp thrill through me, a sinful pleasure that makes my body long for more. I hollow my cheeks, firming my lips around him as I glide up and down his shaft, working him with a paced, hungry rhythm. I want more. I want his control, his dominance—I want him to yank my hair so hard it nearly rips from my scalp.

I want Xan to ruin me.

"I swear to fucking God, there is no way this is real," he groans, his muscles tensing as pleasure wracks through him.

I can feel it—he's close. I give him no reprieve, determined to shatter his restraint. His head tilts downward, his dark eyes locking onto mine, and the moment stretches between us, electric, primal.

I wish I could fully see his face, watch every reaction as control slips away. Instead, I keep fixing his gaze so he can see the silent promise in mine—I want to wreck him as much as he is wrecking me.

"You look so fucking beautiful with my cock in your mouth, little fox," he rasps.

My body trembles at his saying. Each syllable is a balm over the open wounds of today, a twisted comfort in the chaos. My fingers dig into his pants for leverage as I take him even deeper, until my throat stretches around him.

"Don't be afraid. I know you can take it."

He is hanging by a thread, dangling at the threshold of surrender. He thrusts forward, the motion rough enough to make my throat clench, my gag reflex kicking in. Panic flares for a brief second, but his hand in my hair, his voice, his presence—all of it anchors me. I adjust, pushing past the instinct to resist.

"Such a good girl," he murmurs. "I told you—I knew you could take it."

A rush of pride floods me, heady and bewitching. I have control.

Xan may be the one gripping my hair, but I still hold the reins. I decide when and how he will break.

"Show me, little fox. Show me how much you love this. How much you need my cock to fill you in."

I obey without thinking, pressing him even deeper, until tears spill freely from my eyes—not from pain, from the sheer force of it all. I am lost in this, lost in him. I suck harder, faster, desperate for his release, for the final moment that will shatter both of us.

His entire body tenses, his breath coming in ragged gasps as his composure crumbles. He tilts his head back as he finally gives in. Heat floods my mouth, thick and hot, spilling past my lips even as I try swallow every drop.

"Fuck—" he exhales, his voice wrecked, heavy with content. "I didn't think you could get any more beautiful, but with my cum dripping down your face? You're fucking breathtaking."

A deep sigh escapes him, the tension melting from his body.

He is spent. And I am satisfied.

Chapter 13

XAN

I did not have to force her into the shower this time. She went willingly, her body visibly more at ease now. It is a first for me too—this strange feeling crawling under my skin, beyond hatred. I have known respect for Lucian, but never warmth, attachment.

Feelings have no place in my world. However, with Mira... it's hitting differently. Do I like it? I don't know. Yet it's refreshing, like stepping into the chilly night air after being locked in a suffocating room for too long.

Maybe I am capable of redemption after all.

Maybe.

I left her alone, giving her space to gather herself, while I made sure to leave the door slightly ajar. There is no chance in hell I will let her out of my sight. She is my main mission.

I watch from the central room, sprawled in a leather chair, a glass of whisky in one hand, a cigarette burning between my fingers. It is unclear if she knows I am watching; chances are, she wouldn't care.

My breath stutters the moment my eyes land on her. She moves with deliberate grace, dabbing a towel over every inch of her body, her skin still flushed from the hot water. The curve of her waist, the arch of her back—every part of her is temptation itself, a siren built to ruin men.

And fuck, do I want to be ruined.

She slips into the white shirt I left out for her; the fabric swallowing her frame, hiding what I want to see. She tosses the towel aside, letting her damp, fiery hair cascade over her shoulder, water trickling down the curve of her collarbone. She steps out of the bedroom, hesitant, eyes darting around the unfamiliar space.

She is afraid. As she should be. Nothing here is familiar, nothing offers her comfort. Her gaze finally lands on me, and a glimpse of recognition—of relief—softens her expression. A small smile tugs at her lips.

"Come here." I don't ask. I *command.*

She obeys, moving cautiously, still observing every corner of the room.

"You are safe here."

She perches on the chair across from mine, legs crossed, hands tucked beneath her thighs. We stare at each other in silence as the liquor burns its way down my throat. She wants to say something but hesitates. She reaches out—wordlessly asking for my cigarette. Normally, I would not allow it. I hate seeing my girl do something so self-destructive. But considering the events of today, I let it slide.

"Is this... where you live?"

A quiet laugh escapes me. *Live?*

"The Order is my home. I live where my target takes me."

I let the words slip on purpose. I need her to trust me, need her to believe this is mutual. If I want answers, she must think I am giving her something in return. Her brows pull together slightly.

"The Order... They are the ones making you watch me?"

She takes a long drag; the cigarette crackling softly between her fingers.

"At first, yeah. But now... let just say there is a lot more personal interest involved."

I drain the rest of my glass, the dull thud of the empty tumbler against the table filling the silence. She exhales, a ghost of smoke curling through the air as she blows it directly into my face before giving it back.

I keep my composure. That's what she wants, and I do not give people what they want so easily. I have been trained to be cold, controlled, untouchable. Even when control is the hardest thing to hold onto.

"I suppose if I ask why you were watching me, you won't answer?"

Too much attitude. She is right, though. I cannot tell her. Despite that, I also cannot leave without the answers I came here for. Maybe she won't be any more willing to answer me than I am her.

"Let's play a game, little fox." I lean forward. "I will ask you questions. If you answer them correctly..." I pause, drinking in the way she falters. "... I will reward you."

"What kind of reward?," she says with a note of suspicion.

I let my lips curve into an unreadable smile.

"Answer correctly, and you'll find out."

Her brow arches, skepticism tightening her features. Unfazed, she stands her ground. She wants to know.

Good.

I lean back, stretching the silence before speaking again.

"Let us begin. The painting you were obsessing over the other night, right before closing the gallery—the one I gently recreated for you in that little gift you found at your door."

Mira stiffens, looking to her palm. She traces the faint fresh wound carved into her skin, a brand she can never wash away.

"How could I forget?" she says, edged with dry sarcasm. "You made sure I never would."

"What does that illustration mean to you?"

My tone is light, though the intention behind the question is crushing. She lets out a deep exhale. When she finally speaks, her words are brittle, drifting.

"A dream. One I have had for years. Too vivid to be a dream, too fractured to be real." She falters, fingers twitching. "It's always the same. Over and over. Like something trying to claw its way back into my memory."

A cold ripple runs through me, but I force myself to stay still.

"And?"

She lifts her head, a hollow void creeping into her expression.

"It is the only thing I have left of my father."

The room gets dangerously small. A beat passes, then another. The walls feel closer. I don't like it.

Before I can think, I'm standing. Moving. Closing the space between us with eager, measured steps. My fingers find her chin, urgently tilting it upward.

"Tell me what happens in the dream. Every detail."

She smiles, lazy and taunting. "How about my reward?"

The moment fractures. Whatever game we were playing is gone. My hand claws her face, voice sinking lower.

"Forget the reward." The words scrape out, raw and unyielding. "Tell me what you see."

The teasing vanishes. "I—I don't know. It's always so unclear, I can't just—"

A sharp breath burns through my lungs. The frustration inside me snaps like a wire stretched too tight. My palm collides with the armrest of her chair, the impact rattling through the room. She flinches from shock, but I don't care. I lean in, jaw clenched.

"You will remember, Mira. Because if you don't, I will put you in a fucking bunker where no one can ever reach you until you do. Do you understand me?"

Her pulse kicks against the fragile skin of her throat. She swallows, chest rising and falling unevenly. She keeps her stance; she understands the importance. A deep breath shudders through her, her fingers curling against the fabric of her shirt.

"There's an alley." Her voice is barely there. "Dark. Cold. I think it's in the city. Every time I dream of it, I feel this unbearable weight—like grief pressing down on my ribs. Like I'm losing him all over again." She blinks, expression tightening. "Which is totally senseless. He died in a work accident. That is what I was told."

It takes the sting of my nails digging into my palms to notice my hands have clenched into fists.

A pause. Her lips part, but for a moment, nothing comes. Then—"In my dream, it's different... Julian always told me I was imagining things. That it was just my mind playing tricks on me."

A sharp inhale, as if the air itself is cutting into her lungs.

"But after tonight... I don't know what to believe anymore." She blinks rapidly, but not fast enough to stop the tears from rising.

Something inside me twists. It should not. But it does.

"What else? Tell me what happens in the alley right fucking now, Mira."

"There... There's a man." Her breathing shudders. "I never see his face. Though I hear something. A voice, maybe. No, not a voice. A whisper."

The blood in my veins turns to ice.

She presses a hand to her temple, as if trying to physically drag the thought out. "It always ends before I can see more. But tonight... when you mentioned the painting, I felt different. Like I'm supposed to remember. Like I have to."

Silence swells between us. She speaks without knowing. The truth is right there, and she walks right past it. But I see it for what it is. This vision isn't a dream. It's a memory.

And if she remembers the rest—She's dead.

Chapter 14

MIRA

I wake up in the small bed of the unfamiliar room, alone and disoriented, my mind heavy with the thought of last night. Reality hits. I'm in the warehouse, wide awake.

I shift under the blanket, my body stiff, my mind sluggish, and it all comes crashing back. The blood. The violence. The way Julian's betrayal cut deeper than any blade ever could.

I really watched a man have his eye torn from its socket and I really heard Julian barter my life away like a cheap commodity, all for the promise of power. The man I once saw a future with— the one I foolishly believed could have been my husband, even the father of my children—had discarded me like trash.

Now, I am here. Trapped in a place I don't recognize, under the control of a man I can't predict, feeling like prey in a den of wolves.

I push myself upright, running a hand down my face while an intriguing scent stops me. No—multiple scents. Toasted sesame. Rich, dark coffee. The buttery warmth of something sweet—muffins, maybe. Or chocolate. Beneath them all, threading through the air, is a scent that makes between my thighs prickle and my pulse waver.

Xan. Deep, masculine, and unmistakably intoxicating.

I only notice I have moved once I'm already on my feet, ghosting over the cold floor, drawn toward the slightly ajar bathroom door. The steam curls lazily through the gap, carrying heat and the crisp, sharp scent of soap. And through that narrow sliver of space—I see him.

His reflection in the mirror—his bare torso, the tattoos winding across his skin like stories etched in ink. More than that, I see the scars. Raised and jagged, some faint with time, others still exposed. I wonder how many battles he has survived. How many times he has bled and healed. My fingers twitch at my sides, a strange compulsion rising. I want to touch them. To trace the lines of his pain with my own hands.

I should look away. But I remain fixed. I swallow hard, my breath unsteadies as I watch him rake his fingers through his wet hair, slicking it back, exposing the strong cut of his jaw. The water trails down each sculpted line, following the defined ridges of his spine, disappearing over the curves of his waist, his hips, his...—

The door creaks. A single betraying sound. Xan freezes. The bar of soap slips from his grasp, landing with a dull thud against the porcelain. Every muscle in his back locks, his entire body going rigid. His shoulders tense, the slight tilting of his head. The air in the room turns razor-sharp.

Shit.

"Mira..." His tone is a low, deadly warning. "Get. The. Fuck. Out."

I stumble back, my heart hammering. As I turn, my eyes catch on his mask, lying on the counter near the sink. My stomach drops. I almost saw his face. I lunge for the bedroom door, my fingers curling around the handle—it refuses to budge.

Panic flares, sharp and sudden. I try again. It won't turn. I am trapped. I startle as the bathroom door swings open behind me. That's when I see him. Towering. Dripping wet. Naked.

His body gleams under the dim light, every defined muscle of his abdomen chiseled in stark relief, water trailing slow, sinuous paths down the sharp cut of his hipbones, disappearing into the shadows below. His mask is back in place—shielding his identity, guarding whatever secrets lurk beneath. But nothing hides the rigid length of him.

Thick. Hard. Indisputable.

A single breathless second passes. Then another. The air between us crackles like a live wire. Xan tilts his head slightly, voice laced with mischief.

"Well, well." A slow smirk ghosts in his gaze. "You already have your mouth open. Saves me the trouble."

The words snap me out of my trance.

"You know it is not very nice to spy on people, little fox?" A sharp, dry laugh spills from me, jagged and mocking.

"You are out of your fucking mind if you think you get to lecture me about spying, Xan. You, of all people."

The slap comes fast. A sharp, biting crack against my cheek. But I don't flinch. Instead, I lift my chin, meeting his eyes through the mask, my breath trembling, still my resolve unwavering.

His tongue drags lazily over his teeth, his fingers flexing at his sides.

"I like girls with fire," he muses, absentmindedly.

His hand lifts, threading through my hair—gentle for a heartbeat. A brutal yank. I gasp as I am dragged forward, forced onto my knees, his grip unrelenting, his other hand wrapping around his cock, stroking himself with a slow, controlled motion.

"But not when I'm already seconds from bursting."

He grips my hair tightly, his movements forceful as he presses himself deeper, the action coming in sharp, relentless thrusts. I'm surprised at first, but a part of me, perhaps the more primal side, adjusts swiftly.

I lift my head, locking it with his. I want Xan to understand— really understand—that I am not some fragile thing, easily overpowered. That I am not just a victim in this twisted dance. I can be strong. I will not always let him win.

To my surprise, his grip loosens. Slowly, the force in his fingers fades, replaced by a surprisingly gentle touch against my scalp. His hand runs through my hair, soft and almost affectionate. I try to decipher what this shift means in his eyes, but before I can understand, his head tilts back, his body arching with a quiet groan of satisfaction.

The room seems to shrink, and all I can focus on is the contrast between his intense, controlled movements and the fleeting tenderness that I'm not sure he wants to acknowledge.

His breath quickens as I move with a new sense of purpose, feeling him unraveling, bit by bit. The tension builds, a slow burn, as his words slip from his lips, the finality of them sinking in deep.

He's marking me, claiming me in a way I cannot ignore. Despite everything, despite how I have fought to maintain control, I know now I am losing myself in him.

"Fuck," he rasps. His fingers flex against my scalp, not to restrain—just to anchor. "You feel so good, Mira."

I drag my tongue along his length, savoring every pulse, every sharp inhale, every small, ruined sound that escapes him. His head falls back further. A deep, wrecked groan rumbles in his chest.

"You belong to me, little fox. Your mouth to my cock. Your soul to me."

The moment shatters. His hips tense. His body jerks. A hoarse curse rips from his throat as heat floods my mouth, thick and heady. I swallow, my fingers digging into his thighs, my heartbeat thrumming as his body slowly unwinds. His torso heaves, breathing ragged.

Xan's hand tilts my chin up, his thumb brushing over my jaw. A whisper-soft touch. Deadly in its finality.

"I swear to you, Mira—" A slow, possessive caress. "You will never put your lips on another man again."

His grip tightens.

"And that's not a threat."

His voice dips lower.

"It's a fucking promise."

$\mathcal{C}$hapter 15

XAN

$\mathcal{T}$he scent of fresh bagels, coffee, and muffins fills the air. I grabbed literally everything I knew she might enjoy that was fresh from the corner store while she was still asleep this morning. After a night like yesterday, she must be starving, and that is only fair.

I let her have a moment with her breakfast, the silence almost peaceful as I pull on a pair of black jeans and a hoodie, the fabric cool against my skin. I adjust my watch, trying to ignore the gnawing feeling that is building in my chest. It is still early, but there is no time for complacency. Just as I slip my phone into my pocket, it vibrates.

The Order. Now.

That plain text does not leave room for interpretation. Lucian's message is clear, and nothing about it feels good.

After everything Mira dropped on me yesterday, I had not reported back to the Ruler. I had been trying to piece things together, understanding her and the madness that's been unraveling. But his patience has run out. He wants answers, and I am not in a position to deny him.

I crack my neck, the tension in my spine like a coil about to break. I straighten myself up, the pressure of the decision bearing down on me. There is no backing out now. The anger bubbling under my skin has nowhere to go but forward. My mind races, still my body is already moving before I can even think. There is no time left for contemplation. No time for doubt.

I *must* go.

I shove my phone into my pocket, my pulse hammering against my ribs like a war drum.

The Order. Now.

Lucian never texts like that unless shit is about to go sideways. Which means I have a fucking problem.

Last night, I kept my mouth shut. About the way my entire world shifted the second I realized what she might remember. I thought I had time to figure this out before he caught on. Clearly, I was wrong.

Mira is still at the table, picking at her food not having a single damn clue that her life is hanging by a thread. That I might walk out this door and come back with orders to kill her.

A muscle ticks in my jaw. It makes no sense to care. I should have left her in that parking lot. Should have let Julian trade her like the disposable pawn she was supposed to be.

But I did not. And now, I am the one in the goddamn crosshairs.

I take a step toward her, dropping a hand onto the back of her chair, my fingers gripping the wood so tightly my knuckles turn white. She stills instantly. Her body reacts before her brain does—like some deep, buried part of her already knows how men like me operate.

I hate that. I hate the flicker of wariness in her eyes. Hate that I might deserve it.

"I have to go."

She looks up at me, lips parting, hesitation flickering across her face.

"Where?"

"Work."

Her brows pinch together. She wants to push, already knowing I won't let her. She is getting too good at reading me. I don't have time for this. I push off the chair, turn on my heel. But her voice stops me cold.

"Xan..." Just my name. Soft.

I grip the doorknob so hard it nearly breaks. If I look back now, I might not leave. And if I don't leave, Lucian will come looking for me. So, I step out without another word. And slam the door behind me.

———— 🐾 ————

I cut the engine. The car comes to a stop with a low rumble, yet it's the silence that suffocates me. Lucian fucking knows. Or at least, he knows something important. I have no doubt he's been watching. He always does.

That's the thing about him—he plays with people like they are pieces on a board, shifting them into place before they even realize they are in a game. I was meant to be ahead of this. Told him something before he had to summon me like a disobedient dog. But last night... last night changed everything.

Mira.

The way she looked at me, unguarded. The way she took me in her mouth, never breaking eye contact, daring to lose control. She knew exactly what kind of goddamn monster I am and still did not flinch. Fuck, for a moment, I let myself believe she was *really* mine. But Lucian won't see it that way. He will see it as a weakness. A liability.

I roll my shoulders, trying to shake the tension, even so it's useless. She should belong to me. She *does* belong to me. I will be damned if I let him take her away from me.

I move toward the entrance of the compound, the eyes of the others on me. No one says a word. I can feel them judging, but none of them dare to confront me. They know better.

Arriving at his office, I enter without knocking, knowing damn well Lucian's waiting. As soon as I step inside, he looks at me over with that smug smile readable even under his mask, the one that says he already knows exactly how things are going to go. His gaze is sharp, studying me, slicing through the tension like a blade. I can feel the weight of his eyes, calculating, waiting for the perfect moment to strike.

"I have to say, I expected better from you, Xan."

There is a smooth, amused edge to him—masking something cold. The power that comes from a man who owns everything in his sight and relishes every second of it. He takes a measured sip of his drink, placing the glass back on the table with a deliberate clink, the sound cutting through the air.

"You were always my most disciplined one. My most ruthless," he continues, his eyes glinting with satisfaction. "Yet, one little redhead bitch bats her lashes at you, drops down on her knees, and suddenly you're losing your fucking mind."

My jaw tightens. I can feel my fists clench at my sides, the pressure building. I'm pissed—hell, I'm more than pissed. The Ruler exhales sharply through his nose, shaking his head as though he's disappointed by a foolish child.

"She played you like a goddamn instrument, boy," he says, his voice thick with derision. "You think you've tamed her? That you've marked her?"

His grin stretches, turning cruel. "No. She's marking you—and your dick makes you too fucking blind to see it."

I can feel the fury boiling inside me like an explosive volcano, but I hold it in check, focusing on breathing, on staying calm. Lucian leans forward now, elbows resting on the desk with a thud.

"If she can do this to you, imagine what she could do to me."

His eyes flicker for a split second—something dark and unreadable crosses his expression. But it's gone just as quickly as it appeared. He leans back, watching me closely. I know that look. He is enjoying this—enjoying seeing me unravel just a little.

"Tell me, son," he asks, tilting his head, "I heard she kept her eyes locked on yours the whole time she was blowing your dick like the little slut she is, never flinching. I wonder, Xan. Do you really think you're special, or is that just some cute trick she plays with the hundreds of men she gets on the floor for?"

I move before I can stop myself, the chair scraping across the floor, the sound like nails on a chalkboard. My pulse pounds in my throat, my body taut with rage. I don't even know what to say, but I'm already reacting, every fiber of me screaming to lash out.

Lucian remains still. He just watches me, eyes wide with enjoyment. If anything, he looks fucking pleased—he's got me exactly where he wanted. A chuckle escapes his mask, low and mocking, rolling from his chest like it is the sweetest fucking music to his ears.

"You have been watching her, haven't you?" Lucian says, dripping with sarcasm. "Following her every move, trying to figure out what she knows about the man who died. The one

138

she witnessed getting slaughtered. You have been wondering if she could remember, haven't you? What she might know about that night..."

I stay silent. He's right. I have been digging, following her every step. She has been the key to understanding that event. To understanding what I was a part of, what happened when I was just a fucking kid. The night I watched a man die at the age of 9. The moment Lucian taught me everything I needed to know about the Order, about betrayal.

"Too bad you never stopped to ask the right question," he says slowly, his eyes gleaming with that same cold pleasure that always made me want to break his face. "The question you should have been asking Xan is... who exactly was the man Mira accidently watched die?"

I blink, my thoughts momentarily derailing as something inside me shifts, that gnawing suspicion clawing at the back of my mind. I stare at him, barely able to keep my thoughts together.

"What the hell are you talking about?"

Lucian takes a step closer, his voice lowering to a quiet hiss.

"You never bothered to dig into her past. You were so focused on what she remembered, on what secrets she could uncover, on getting her mouth around your cock, that you did not bother asking the one question that would have changed everything."

My heart is pounding now, my stomach twisting with a familiar anxiety, a sense of dread creeping up my spine.

"Because you were there, Xan. You were there when her father died," Lucian continues, and for the first time in this entire fucked-up conversation, his tone turns sharp, almost cruel. "You saw it with your own eyes, and yet you never connected the dots. You never realized who that man really was, did you?"

I feel like the ground has been pulled out from beneath my feet. My legs almost give way, trying to hold myself steady, clenching my fists at my sides.

"No... That's not possible."

His eyes are a flicker of triumph as he watches me spiral.

"*Oh*, it is possible alright, you just didn't know it at the time. You were too young, too naïve to see it for what it was. But now? Now, you are piecing it together, aren't you? The man you thought was a stranger, the one you saw perish in that cold, bloody night... was Edmund Vale, your sweet little fox's daddy."

I take a step back, my breath catching in my throat. My hands are shaking now, the reality of it crashing over me, the truth sinking in.

I *was* there.

I watched Edmund Vale die.

The man who should have been her protector. The man who... was her father. I stare at Lucian, my chest tightening.

"*You* killed him, not me!"

The words come out like a growl, the accusation hanging in the air. Lucian's smile widens, satisfaction radiating from him like a fucking aura.

"Yes, I killed him. While you, Xan... you watched it happen and did nothing. You were a part of it. We both were and still are."

I try to swallow the lump in my throat, the bitterness of the truth almost choking me. I didn't know. I didn't know who he was to her. My mind is spinning. I cannot process it all at once.

"But why the fuck would you..."

I was just a kid, a witness, nothing more. Another tool in Lucian's hands. Damn, I feel sick.

Lucian steps closer. "Mira's nothing more than collateral damage, Xan. She's a means to an end. She always has been."

I feel the tornado building inside me, but I keep it in check. There is no point in lashing out again, not right now. I need to process this. I need to understand exactly what the hell I am supposed to do with this information. Lucian gives me a look, an egotistic contentment spreading across his face as he leans in closer.

"You see, Xan," he says softly, "Edmund was not just any man. He was my best friend, my closest ally. But he also used to be the Ruler of the Order. The power he held... It was never going to be mine unless he was out of the picture. I just had no choice."

My stomach twists. The pieces fall into place.

"I promised him, Xan. I promised Edmund that I would keep Mira safe, protect her. I also knew that the only way to take his place—truly seize the power of the Order—was to kill him. To destroy every single thing he stood for. To eliminate what could stand in my way. You're getting it now, aren't you?" he sneers. "Edmund had to go—simple as that. He was in my way, and I do not let obstacles linger. As for Mira? Keeping her alive was a debt I agreed to honor. Nothing more. Nothing less. And I'm a man of my word; a promise is a promise."

I can't help but burst into a laugh, on the verge of hysteria, overwhelmed by the rush of revelations flooding my brain.

"You really think that not killing Mira makes you some kind of saint?" I snarl, my voice thick with fury. "You robbed her of any chance to grow up with a father!"

Lucian turns toward me, his supercilious smile unwavering, almost amused.

"You should thank me, Xan! What better way to make her yours? This is a golden opportunity for you to be called 'daddy' when you finally get to fuck her."

Before I can stop myself, my fist flies, crashing into his jaw with a sickening crack. Lucian's head snaps back, but no reaction whatsoever. Does not even raise an eyebrow. He just laughs, the sound sharp and condescending.

"That is all you've got, boy? You really think this changes anything? It doesn't. We have passed the point of no return."

142

I am shaking. I can feel the pulse in my temples, the heat of fury boiling inside. My grip on the knife tightens. I want to bury it in his throat, to watch him bleed for every word he has said. I am so close to explode, the insanity at the brink of my mind.

"Do you want to kill me, Xan?" he asks playfully, clearly amused by my struggle. "You think you can?"

I grind my teeth so hard I'm afraid I will crack them, my breathing ragged, my whole body aching with the need to destroy him.

"Come on, pull yourself together, boy." Lucian's voice drips with condescension, his fun barely masked beneath the razor-sharp edge of his authority. He leans back, utterly relaxed, as if this is just another day at the office for him.

"Thanks to my cameras in the hangar, I gathered she recognizes the alley. That she's making the connection to Edmund. Am I correct?" He pauses, watching me for any reaction. "Is there anything else you might be keeping from me?"

I remain quiet. I can tell his lips are curing into a knowing sneer just by the look in his eyes.

"Let's make a deal, shall we? You keep feeding me the information I want, and in return, we pretend you don't know a damn thing about her father. Not that I imagine you would be rushing to tell her you stood by and watched it happen without lifting a finger, would you?"

His words are poison, each one sinking beneath my skin, corroding whatever restraint I have left.

"And in exchange for your loyalty," he continues smoothly, "I won't send Kayde to fuck Mira before he slices her throat."

That sick cunt. *Kayde*—the bastard who has been waiting for an opportunity to crawl up the ranks. If Lucian gives the order, he will not hesitate. He will break my girl in ways I cannot even fucking imagine. And no matter what I do, no matter how much I try to keep her safe, she will be beyond my reach.

"You don't need Kayde for this," I grit out. "And you damn know it."

Lucian chuckles.

"Good. Then we are in agreement. We will continue this mission in harmony—you keep giving me what I want, and I won't say a word while I watch you rail her through my monitors." He takes a slight pause.

"*Oh*, and don't get mad if I decide to broadcast it across the Order's screens, hmm? Your colleagues had a great time jerking off to her huge tits while she was showering last night."

My vision whites out for a second. My fists clench, nails digging into my palms so hard I might break the skin. He's testing me. Mocking me. Dangling her in front of me like bait, just to see how much I can take before I break.

And I'm *this* close.

Chapter 16

MIRA

Xan opens the door to the hotel room, and the moment I step inside, the grandeur hits me like a tidal wave. He told me the warehouse was not safe anymore. Of course, he won't tell me why. All I know is that he has taken it upon himself to get us out of there and into this place.

A massive suite, more like an entire floor than just a room. I still don't understand what is going on, but my exhaustion from the previous night presses down on me, and I'm too drained to ask questions. I just follow him silently, my body moving on its own, numb to everything else.

When I look around, it is not just a room—it's a statement. The walls are lined with floor-to-ceiling windows, giving a panoramic view of the New York skyline. The city's lights twinkle below, the streets buzzing with life, yet from up here, it all feels so distant, so far away from everything that has happened.

The penthouse is overwhelming in its opulence, with lavish furnishings that seem too extravagant to be real. The kind of place where wealth is not just a fact; it is flaunted in every corner.

In the center of the living room stands a giant jacuzzi and golden statues of leopards are scattered throughout the space, standing guard over the decadent furniture. They are absurdly unnecessary, still they give off this 'too rich for my own good' vibe that, for some reason, appeals to me right now.

I take in the view again. From the 34th floor, the city stretches out beneath me in every direction. It is stunning, almost dizzying. For a brief second, it gives me a sense of peace I have not felt in what feels like forever. The chaos of the past days—hell, the past few years—feels like its miles away. The contrast is almost too much to bear. The calm of the scene clashes with the animosity brewing inside of me, but the sight is soothing in its own way.

As I walk further into the suite, I notice something else. Two separate bedrooms. I glance at Xan, a little confused. The gesture catches me off guard. It is... thoughtful, almost. I cannot remember the last time someone was this considerate, especially him.

"Yours is on the right. I had the hotel prepare clean clothes for you. They should be on the bed."

He moves on before I can respond. He just turns and heads toward the left bedroom, closing the door behind him with a soft click, followed by the unmistakable sound of a lock turning. I am left standing there, staring at the now-locked door, and I get the distinct feeling that I will not see him again anytime soon. He probably wants some time alone, maybe to take off that damn mask and just breathe for a minute. Anyway, I'm not expecting him to come out, and that is fine by me.

I look at the suite again, trying to take it all in, while my attention is drawn back to the jacuzzi. It calls to me, the steam curling up from the water like an invitation to escape. No need to think. No questions to ask. All that matters is letting go.

I peel off the oversized white sweater of his that I have been wearing as a dress, dropping it carelessly onto the floor. The fabric feels too heavy now, and the water is the only thing that promises any kind of relief.

The moment I step into the jacuzzi, the hot liquid wraps around me like a blanket, soothing and intense at the same time. The bubbling heat rushes over my skin, easing away the tension in my shoulders and my back. I sink deeper, the pressure of the world lifting just slightly, enough to make me forget—at least for now. The water is perfect, and the soft jets push against my skin, massaging away the tightness in my muscles.

To my surprise, there is a bottle of champagne waiting for me, chilling in an ice bucket beside the edge. I stare at it for a moment, wondering who would expect such a thing, then realize—of course, the hotel. They must think I am some high-powered businessman's secret mistress, whisked away to a hidden oasis for an illicit affair.

It makes sense, given the level of opulence here—the gold-trimmed furniture, the king-size art pieces hanging on the walls, the ridiculous amount of space that seems designed for people who want to flaunt their wealth. The whole place screams excess, a setting made to impress, to show off. It is all too much, and yet... here I am, dipping deeper into the overindulgence, letting it swallow me whole.

I pick up the champagne to pop the cork, the soft sound almost comforting, and pour myself a glass. The bubbles rise in the crystal-clear beverage, catching the light as they sparkle. I take a sip, the drink cool and crisp, a sharp contrast to the warmth of the water. The sensation fills me, distracting me from the mess of thoughts that swirl in my mind.

For a second, I let myself pretend. Pretend that I am not trapped in this chaotic, dangerous world. Pretend that none of this matters—that it is all just a fleeting moment, one that I can enjoy before the storm comes crashing down again. I take another sip, letting the bubbles dance on my tongue, allowing myself to forget everything.

The water is blistering hot, kissing my skin as I sink further, embracing the pulsing jets kneading at my tense, aching muscles. My head tips back against the marble brink, lips parting as I exhale slowly.

The city sprawls beneath me beyond the window, thousands of tiny lights blinking in the dark. In this moment, I don't care about anything beyond the heat licking at my body and the steady thrum between my legs. I shift slightly, the jet pressing harder against me. *Right there.* A sharp jolt of sensation sparks into my core, and my fingers curl against the ledge.

Fuck.

The pressure is good, relentless, teasing in a way that makes my thighs twitch. It has been too long—too much stress, too much tension coiled tight inside me with nowhere to go. I bite my lip, half in hesitation, half in anticipation, and push my hips forward just a little. Somehow, it is not just the water that is making my body tighten with envy.

It's *him.*

The way his voice drips with command, how his presence alone ignites something dark and unrelenting. The memory of his gloved hands gripping my waist, the rough brush of fabric against my bare skin when he moves too close—he has still never touched me the way I crave, even though my body reacts as if he already has.

The jet pulses directly against my pussy, and I gasp. I part instinctively, welcoming the force, the heat, the way the water licks at my most sensitive spot with a rhythm I don't have to think about.

I picture his eyes—cold, analyzing, always watching. Does he know how badly I want him? How it tortures me, this maddening game of restraint?

My fingers slide down, teasing, exploring, pushing myself closer to that unbearable precipice. My hips grind, seeking more, needing more. A slow, tentative press against the stream as the pleasure intensifies. A delicious tingle spreads through my core, a liquid ache pooling deep in my stomach. My nipples tighten, the contrast of the hot water and cool air only adding to the sensation twisting inside me.

God, that feels good.

If he were here next to me, would he break? Would he finally give in to the hunger I know he buries beneath his mask? Or would he just watch, amused, making me beg before he would even consider touching me?

My breathing is uneven now, every nerve in my body lighting up as I rock forward again, letting the flow hit me just right. My fingers tighten against the marble, my knuckles white as I chase the friction, slow at first, then more desperate. More needy.

The pleasure builds, coiling low in my belly, the steady rush of water unforgiving against my clit. Every shift, every tiny movement sends another jolt through me, winding me tighter, dragging me higher. My legs tremble, my breath catches, my mouth part in a silent moan—So close. I bite my lip, stifling his name before it slips out. At this moment, he's everywhere. In my mind, in my body, in the heat that pulses through me as I finally let go.

Oh, fuck—

The orgasm crashes, violent and sharp, knocking the breath from my lungs as my body locks up. My thighs snap together, a strangled moan tearing from my lips as euphoria detonates, white-hot and all-consuming. My hips jerk involuntarily, my body milking every drop of sensation as aftershocks ripple, making me shudder.

For several beats, I remain still. I just float, chest heaving, the fog swirling lazily around me. My body feels loose, languid, completely spent, and a satisfied smirk tugs at the corner of my lips.

Damn, I *needed* that.

The heat lingers on my skin as I step out of the jacuzzi, water streaming down my legs in glistening rivulets. I wrap myself in the plush towel; the fabric soaking up the moisture as I run a hand through my hair. The high from my earlier indulgence has faded, leaving me restless.

I peek around the penthouse. Luxurious, opulent... and suffocatingly dull. Xan locked himself away without another word. And as much as I appreciate the safety of this gilded cage, I feel like I might go insane if I stay here any longer. I pad barefoot toward the bedroom he designated as mine, pushing open the door.

Just as he promised, a selection of clothes is neatly folded on the bed. Classy, expensive, a little too tailored for my usual style—but beggars can't be choosers. I slip into a silky black dress that hugs my curves, the fabric cool against my heated skin. The neckline plunges just enough to be tempting without screaming desperation, and the hem skims mid-thigh, teasing more than it reveals. A pair of strappy heels waits by the dresser, and I slide them on, reveling in the subtle click they make against the immaculate stonework as I move.

A glance in the mirror confirms what I already know—I look good. More importantly, I look like I belong in a place like this.

I do not bother knocking on Xan's door. If he wanted to be part of my night, he wouldn't have shut me out. Honestly, I don't need him. Instead, I grab my keycard and head straight for the elevator, anticipation humming through my veins.

The bar downstairs is calling my name, and it would be very rude to not answer, *right?*

Chapter 17

MIRA

I step into the elevator, the sleek mirrored walls reflecting the image of a woman who should feel safer, who should feel grateful. Xan gave me this lavish escape, this sanctuary high above the city, yet all I feel is restless. A drab ache of dissatisfaction coils in my stomach, deeper than boredom—much closer to longing.

The hotel bar is haloed in murky light, bathed in a golden glow that makes everything feel slow, hazy, intimate. A grand chandelier hangs above the curved mahogany counter, its crystals reflecting the amber hues of expensive whiskey in crystal glasses. The scent of aged liquor and faint cigar smoke lingers in the air, mixing with the soft notes of a jazz tune humming through the speakers.

I slide onto a green velvet barstool, crossing my legs deliberately, ignoring the way the dress I threw on clings to my damp skin. The bartender approaches, all polished charm and sharp features, offering me a smile that probably works on every woman who walks in alone.

"What can I get for you, Miss?"

I could ask for something strong, something that would burn, but instead, I ask, "Something sweet."

As he nods and moves to prepare my drink, my fingers drum idly against the smooth bar top, my pulse a little too quick, my nerves a little too sensitive.

I have no business being here. I was meant to stay upstairs, in the safety Xan carved out.

Maybe that's the problem. Safety. Controlled environments. Locked doors and dictated choices. I want to feel something else. I want—

The bartender sets the glass in front of me, a cocktail in deep red, garnished with a curl of citrus. I take a slow sip, letting the strawberry warmth settle in my chest. Maybe if I sit here long enough, if I push the boundaries just a little, he will come. I beg myself to stop wanting. But want is written in my skin.

Would he be angry? Would he drag me back upstairs, growling? Or would he stay in the shadows, watching and waiting, letting me churn in my own desire?

I shift in my seat, exhaling sharply. If he won't come, then maybe I will just have to give him a reason to.

The ice in my glass clinks softly as I swirl the crimson liquid inside, my fingers tracing absent patterns along the rim. The hotel bar is barely illuminated, an ambiance of quiet luxury that hums around me, wrapping me in a cocoon of muted conversation and soft music. Though my mind is absent, because it is still upstairs, sealed in that penthouse suite with him. Or rather, it should be. I cannot shake the irrational hope that, any second now, he will appear behind me.

I take another long sip of my drink, my heart quickening at the idea. Again, would he be jealous? Would he yank me from this stool, whisper venomous threats against anyone who even dare look at me? The thought sends a thrill curling low in my stomach. I want him to come and find me. I want to push him. I want to see what it takes to break his self-control.

As if summoned by my thoughts, a figure slides into the seat beside me. My breath stills. Black gloves. Black jacket. Mask. He says nothing. Just reaches for a bottle behind the bar—a movement so casual, so practiced, that it sends a delicious shiver down my spine. Without a word, he pours a glass of a dark smoky drink, setting it before him with a slow motion. I smirk.

"So, you changed your mind?"

Still, he doesn't speak. Instead, he tilts his head slightly, as if studying me and slowly trails his gloved fingers along the stem of my glass before nudging it closer.

A subtle invitation.

My lips part, my tongue flicking out to wet them. He is playing a game. A dangerous one. And I want to play too so badly.

I savor the liquid; my gaze focused on him. He shifts closer, just enough for his knee to brush mine.

The moment lingers. My pulse thrums against my skin. Without a word, he stands and starts walking away. I hesitate for half a second before finally following.

The elevator ride is silent. Tense. His gloved hand presses the button for another floor—not ours. That should give me a pause. Instead, I am drawn forward. I want to see where this leads.

When the doors slide open, he steps out first. I trail after him, biting my nails as we move down a long, dim hallway. The whole thing feels surreal, like I have stepped into someone else's fantasy. He stops in front of a door, swipes a key card, and pushes it open without looking at me. I smirk.

"A second room, huh? Getting creative." No answer.

I step inside, my heels clicking softly against the floor. It is smaller than the penthouse, but still insanely luxurious, the lights lowered to a soft glow. The door shuts behind me, and a thrill of anticipation runs in me.

Without warning, his touch lands on my breast.

I gasp—not surprisingly, but from the sheer urgency in the way he moves. No teasing. Just hunger, hands gripping my waist, pressing me back against the wall, his body flush against mine. A gloved hand skims up my thigh, pushing the fabric of my dress higher. My breath catches.

Still... something feels off. The way he touches me—it is not the same. There is no slow, careful build-up. No controlled dominance. Just impatience.

My fingers grip his wrist.

"You are different tonight," I murmur. "Less... refined."

His head tilts as he finally speaks for the first time of the night.

"Disappointed?"

The voice is wrong.

A chill slams me violently, as if I have been doused in ice water. My stomach clenches. My heart stutters. I shove at his torso, hard. He barely stumbles.

"Take off the mask," I demand.

To my horror, he does—no hesitation. The second the mask is gone, I know. The smirk on his face is cruel, mocking.

Not him. Not him. Not him. That is not Xan.

I turn to run, but he's faster. A hand fists in my hair, yanking me backward. Pain flares down my scalp as I am thrown to the ground, my breath knocking out in a sharp gasp.

As he crawls on my body, I thrash. He grabs my wrists, pinning them above my head, his breath hot against my cheek as he chuckles darkly.

"What's wrong, sweetheart?" while pressing his knee between my thighs. "You looked so eager a second ago."

Panic claws at my throat. I scream. I writhe beneath him, my breath coming in sharp, ragged bursts. His grip tightens around my wrists, his gloved fingers biting into my skin as he leans in closer. I snarl, twisting my body, but his weight is suffocating.

Not him. Not Xan.

"Get the fuck off me!" My voice is a breathless snarl, but it only amuses him.

"Why?" he laughs. "Because I'm not *him, Xan*? Need *his* permission maybe?"

I freeze. His hand drags along the inside of my thigh.

"An anonymous man in a mask," he muses. "Or another. What does it change, really, once you lay on your belly?"

My stomach turns. "Fuck you," I spit, bucking hard against him. His hold tightens, but I see it now—that flicker of thrill in his expression, the power trip. He thinks he has already won.

Fool.

I throw my knee up, aiming for anything I can reach. Expecting it, his hand catches my thigh, squeezing hard enough to make me wince. He leans in, his breath warm and vile against my ear.

"Come on baby, you came here looking for a masked man to wreck you. Does it really matter which one it is? Just close your eyes and let a real man finally rail you how you have been craving."

I should have never dared challenge life like this. I should have listened to Xan, stayed in the safety of his presence, let him protect me like he always promised.

But no, I had to push; I had to test the limits and now look at me—trapped in this goddamn nightmare, tangled in my own mess.

I hate the place I'm in right now, the helplessness that is creeping in. More than anything, I hate myself for stepping so far into danger, for thinking that I could play with fire and not get burned. I hate myself for ever believing he would always be there to pull me from the flames, to save me from whatever I got myself into.

Because now I see—he is not here, and I am completely fucking alone.

The rush of blood in my ears drowns everything else out. My limbs lock up. My stomach is lurching. I fucked up. His hold crushes my arm, yanking me closer. I jerk back, twisting hard, but he's stronger. The back of my head slams against the wall, pain exploding through my skull. He moves in, pressing me into the door, his knee nudging between my thighs.

"Relax. You were willing a second ago? Why stop now?"

I swing. Hard. My palm connects with his face, nails dragging across his skin. He curses, gripping my jaw so tight my teeth ache. "Feisty." He licks the blood from his lip. "But not for long." My pulse slams against my ribs as he reaches for his belt.

Fuck. Fuck. Fuck.

My brain scrambles for a way out, but before I can move, the door explodes open. A blur of black. A thunderous impact. The man is ripped off me so violently he barely has time to make a sound before he is crashing into the dresser, the lamp shattering on the floor.

Xan.

I lurch away as I watch Xan completely unravel with just raw, unfiltered brutality. Every hit is intense, purposeful, designed to break. Blood splatters across the pristine carpet, staining it in chaotic patterns. A wet, choking sound escapes the man's throat, his attempts to shield himself growing weaker with each impact. He is barely conscious, his face swollen and unrecognizable.

Clearly, Xan gives zero fucks.

He's going to kill him.

Stopping him crosses my mind. So does speaking up. However, all I can do is stare, my breath shallow, my body trembling. Xan finally exhales, his shoulders rising and falling like a tempest barely contained. His knuckles are drenched in red as he finally lifts his gaze to mine. His mask is still in place, but his presence—his fury—is animalistic.

He steps closer angrily.

"You think you can just fucking wander off?"

I open my mouth, but no words come. I don't know what to say.

I wanted you to follow me? I wanted to see if you would come after me?

He grabs my chin violently, forcing me to meet his gaze.

"Say something now," he demands roughly.

I stay speechless. Because the only thing I can focus on right now is the way my body reacts—how, despite the terror, I want him. Right here, in the wreckage of this room, with anger still thrumming in his veins and blood staining his knuckles.

I want him to take me, to claim me in the chaos he created, to make me feel every ounce of the rage that is still burning beneath his skin. I want him to show me what *defying Xan* truly means. To make me understand just how much this pushed him past his breaking point. To punish me for thinking, even for a second, that I could walk away from him.

Still unable to form a single word, I reach out, my fingers trembling as they move toward his face. He grabs my wrist in an instant, his grip savage, unyielding.

"Don't."

The command is guttural, but I fight against his hold, forcing him to loosen his grip just enough for me to slip through. My fingers find his hair—dark, unruly, still damp with blood. His blood. Someone else's. I don't care.

I stroke a tangled strand, watching the red smear across my fingertips, staining them with evidence of his violence. It fascinates me. Hypnotizes me. I stare at my hand as if it holds the answer to unspoken secrets, as if it might unlock some deep, forbidden truth between us.

I know he is watching me. Studying me just as intently. I want him to understand that I am not afraid of his fury.

I crave it.

Steadily, I draw my hand back, trailing it down the dainty strap of my satin dress. I let it slip from my shoulder, exposing the curve of my skin beneath. His breath shudders, ragged and heavy. That's when I see it—the way his cock twitches, thickening right before my eyes. My bloodstained fingers glide over my bare shoulder, down the slope of my collarbone, and across the swell of my breast, leaving streaks of crimson in their wake. A silent offering. A challenge.

Look, Xan. Look at what you make me do.

At how I come undone for you, how I sink willingly into this dark, twisted devotion. How I want you to keep spilling his blood until there is nothing left, until the room reeks of death, and you know—you fucking know—that no other man can ever touch me without paying the price with his life. I want you to destroy anyone who dares lay eyes on me. I want you to find me and break me repeatedly until I am nothing but yours. Forever.

I reach up, fingers tracing the sharp line of his jaw under his mask, feeling the tension coiled beneath his skin. He's still furious. Still lost in whatever is raging inside him. My other hand drags lower, smearing streaks of blood across my own flesh. It is written all over his eyes—the way he follows the movement, his pupils blown wide with desire beyond lust.

"You're still thinking about him," he says roughly.

I shake my head, nails digging into his shoulder.

"What, no!"

"Liar." His fingers tighten around my wrist, pinning me. "You let him touch you."

I cannot believe what I'm hearing.

"Oh my God, stop, I thought it was you!"

His grip shifts, pushing my wrist above my head, stretching me beneath him on the floor until I am fully at his mercy.

"I don't give a fuck even if you though I was the fucking pope." His lips graze my ear. "You belong to me."

All I long to tell him is that he is right, that he has conquered me in every way, that I am his now. That my heart bears his mark as clearly as my arm, indelibly stained with his presence, with his claim. I offer myself to him—surrendering in exchange for comfort, protection, and the promise of love that feels as tangled and consuming as the maelstrom he stirs within me.

I am still adrift in the uncertainty of whether I am nothing more than an object for him to possess—an item in his psychotic collection. Deeper still, I wonder if he can hold me close in any form other than the suffocating grip of ownership and dominance.

My devotion to him would be boundless, but he must show me, in the quiet spaces between us, that I am more than a mere possession. That I am worthy beyond the cold distance of control—that I am, in the end, real, *human*. Only then will I surrender fully, heart and soul. Until that moment, I remain lost in the swirling uncertainty of what he genuinely wants from me.

Xan senses the shift in my attitude immediately. I see it in the rigid set of his shoulders; in the way his breath slows. Just as swiftly, he pulls away. He steps back as if shrugging off an unwelcome weight, a presence he no longer wants.

Me.

Without a word, he pivots toward the door, his movements clipped, decisive. Confusion flares in my chest.

"That's it? We're just leaving him here?"

He turns his head slightly, unreadable, as if my question were no more than idle small talk.

"You're right."

Reaching into his pocket, he withdraws a thick stack of cash and tosses it onto the bed. The bills land like fallen leaves over the crimson-soaked sheets, soft, indifferent to the ruin beneath them. His phone is already in hand, his fingers moving with that same calculated ease. A muted voice crackles through the receiver.

"Room 592. Floor 28. Premium cleaning." Flat. Unbothered.

He ends the call without ceremony, tucking the phone away, and strides toward the exit without so much as a peek in my direction.

"Are you staying the night? Because I doubt he's in any shape to make you come."

The words are venomous, laced with anger, even jealousy. But it is the insinuation that makes my blood boil. After everything, he is still questioning whether I wanted that man's touch. He still sees possibilities where there should absolutely be none. I exhale, pressing against the weight of my exhaustion, my frustration. Yet bitterness festers. Festers and rots.

"Funny. I think I'd have a better chance of coming with a corpse than with you."

The second the words settle into the room, I know I have left a wound. Yet no reaction. No flare of anger. No flicker of suffering.

Nothing.

His stare is hollow, endless, gazing into the mouth of an abyss. Without another word, he turns, stepping into the hallway. His departure is a careful, unhurried severing. Just as he crosses the threshold, I hear it—so quiet I almost miss it.

"Should have left her to him."

Chapter 18

XAN

I stalk down the corridor, every step reverberating with the sting of my own words, circling back, growing heavier, sharper, sinking their claws into me like a curse I can't shake.

Betrayal.

I should have slammed her down. Pressed her into the unforgiving floor, wrists crushed beneath my grip, her body convulsing under the raw violence she dared to summon. I should have torn through her defiance, skin blooming purple beneath my hands, blood smearing under my fingers like war paint. I should have marked her—bruised, bitten, bleeding—until her screams turned to silence, until the lesson etched itself into the marrow of her bones turning the soft curve of her butt a furious shade of red. Again. And again. Until nothing remained but obedience and the echo of my name in her throat.

You don't get to speak to me like that.

Not when I am tearing apart every damn thing I have ever known for you. Not when I am fucking unraveling at the seams for you.

Every reckless word, every ounce of defiance, every fucking wound she has carved into me. Let her wear it in the bruises I would have given her, in the heat of my palm against her flesh, in the way her breath would catch when she realized—there is no escaping me. No running from the madness she has stirred in my blood.

Even though, I let her stand there with that bitchy mouth that cuts like a blade, those eyes that gut me deeper than any knife ever could.

It is not too late to turn back, Xan.

The thought slams into me like a command, an inevitability. My body stills, muscles coiled so tight they ache.

No. She does not get to fuck with my head and leave as if it was all a game. She started this—she can damn well deal with the fallout. Especially when I just had to kill a man to save her ungrateful ass.

My hands tighten into fists. My teeth grind. I turn. with cold, brutal certainty.

I stalk back to the door, pushing it open so forcefully it crashes against the wall before I kick it shut behind me. The sound cracks through the room like a gunshot. Mira has not moved, still standing there as if she was waiting—no, hoping—that

I would come back for her. The way her lips twitch, with just the faintest hint of relief, makes my blood burn hotter.

Sorry, little fox.

"You think this is over?" My voice drops, sharp and unforgiving. "The bed. On your fucking stomach. Now."

Her expression shifts instantly. Confusion first. Then realization. And finally, fear.

Perfection.

She stands, her posture rigid, but halts mid-motion.

"Okay, Xan. I'm sorry for what I said, truly. But the bed... it's soaked in blood, and there is an entire man's body lying there..." I let out a soft, bitter laugh.

"Even better. After that, you would have to be fucking stupid to try that shit again. But hey—maybe you *want* to get ruined. Maybe that filthy little mouth of yours was begging for it."

My words are void of mercy, devoid of any compassion. She thought that man was me. I can see that now. A misunderstanding, fine. But the way she answers, the way she brushes it off—it is unforgivable, especially after everything I have sacrificed to keep her alive.

She remains unmoved. Silent rebellion. And just like that, she pushes me past the line. No more mercy.

"You wanted to lie down with him? Here's your chance, baby girl."

In a single, controlled motion, I seize her, shoving her face-first onto the mattress. She cries out, but it means nothing to me. She should have thought about this before she spoke. Her body is trembling, stiff with defiance and desperation.

I grip her wrist hard, forcing her back onto the bed as she gasps, her eyes wide with shock. It makes no difference. Nothing matters except this—making her understand, feel every ounce of anger that I have been building inside.

"You thought you could say whatever the hell you wanted and get away with it? After everything I've fucking done for you?"

She flinches, but it is too late. I yank her closer, making her face me, forcing her to look me in the eye as I speak.

"You wanted to cross a line, *huh*? You wanted to test me? You have no idea what you've done, Mira."

Her breath catches as I press my body closer, pinning her down with a suffocating intensity. There is no escape. She cannot run from me now.

"I've kept you alive. I've kept you safe," I snarl. "And this is how you repay me? With your fucking attitude and your pathetic little games!"

Her pulse quickens, her chest heaving beneath me, I can tell she is feeling it now. The heat. The anger. I grab her by the chin, drawing her into my stare, to see each single drop of hatred and desire mixing inside my body.

"Looking for pain, were you? Well, here it is. Here's what happens when you push me too far. So desperate to make me look at you. You've got my attention now and you're going to regret to be alive."

I cut her off before she speaks.

"If I did not have this mask on, Mira, I would kiss you so fucking brutally you would not be able to breathe. Your entire face would feel the burn of my rage as I would sink my teeth into your lips until I taste the blood seeping into my mouth."

She is trembling underneath me, teetering on the edge of a breakdown or a revelation.

Good. That is exactly what I want.

"You think I'm a monster, Mira?" I ask, "Because you do not know what monsters are capable of."

Her breath hitches again, and I can see the struggle in her eyes—part of her still wants to fight, but the rest of her knows I am not playing anymore.

Every inch of me is focused on her—on the way she is reacting, the way she is fighting it even though she craves it. The way her eyes are still burning with defiance, even though they are caught in my grip.

"You believe you know what you want? What does it mean to push me to this point?"

She tries to look away, but I stop her. I force her to stay with me, in the storm we have created.

"You asked for this side of me, for the beast you think I am." I whisper. "Don't be so sure you will survive it."

Her chest is rising faster, and I see the fight leave her eyes. I let go of her chin, my fingers trailing down her neck, feeling the quick beats of her pulse. My hand pauses at the base of her throat, pressing down just enough to make her gasp.

"I know you are just dying to make me lose control."

She shakes her head. I can feel her submission, her surrender, even if she is still trying to deny it. Her mouth parts, her breath is shallow. I know—deep down—that she wants it. Wants *me*. Wants to feel this power, this dominance, though it terrifies her.

"Say it," I say in a dark and dangerous way. "Say you want me, say you *need* me. Because there is no turning back now. Once I've taken you, you will never be the same."

I see it in her eyes—the vulnerability, the pure desire that has been buried beneath all her resistance. It is like a switch flipped, and she is no longer fighting me. She is giving in, whether she likes it or not. Damn, I cannot hold back anymore.

I lean down. "You're mine now, little fox. You're mine to break. And I'll break you, piece by piece, until there is *nothing* left but the echo of what I've done."

I take the time to turn her head toward the body lying beside her. I want her to look at her mistake, to realize the extent of all her actions, as foolish as they may have been.

My hands move over her, fingers dragging along the curve of her hips before I tear the satin dress from her body, stripping her bare to my sight. A sharp inhale, her spine bowing, her skin rising in goosebumps—she feels it. The danger. The inevitable.

I seize her ass with both hands, digging in hard, not caring if it hurts—only that she won't forget the way it felt. She lets out a strangled gasp as her thighs clench shut, caught between pain and craving.

She thought playing with fire would be fun. Now she will learn what it means to burn.

Chapter 19

MIRA

What have I done with my life to end up here, caught in this spiraling chaos of degradation and torment?

I close my eyes, trying to escape the gravity of this reality crushing me, still each image cuts deeper, more relentless. Just days ago, I was content, immersed in the calm of my art gallery, a world where the frenzy of the outside world felt distant, almost unreal.

I advised wealthy clients, those hollow beings who wandered in, desperate to adorn their meaningless lives with something of value. I watched as the Victorias complimented paintings they did not understand, pretending they had passions beyond their wealth and gossip. Meanwhile, their Reginalds played the part of attentive husbands, offering polite 'yes, yes' and 'no, no,' when in truth, their minds were elsewhere—thinking of Chloe, the little escort they'd just spent the night with, relishing the fleeting connection that felt more real to them than the stale lives they led.

I had always found it all so absurd, and yet, in this moment, I ache for it—the ridiculousness of it all. My pretentious clients, their empty compliments, their hollow chatter about things they could never truly grasp. I miss the laughter with Zoey, the quietude of my apartment, untouched by the storm that now tears through my life. I miss the monotony, the simplicity of it.

Could Xan really live amidst such banality? To wake up one morning with nothing more than the soft light of dawn spilling over the floor, a dog at his feet, a cup of coffee warming his hands, and a book in his lap as he watches the world go by through a window.

The thought feels oneiric. He is made for danger, for things that thrive in the shadows. Still, in these moments with him, I see a side of myself I never knew existed—fragments of who I am, now awakened from a long slumber. It is as though he is peeling back layers of me I thought I had buried, and with each revelation, I am caught between resistance and surrender.

I am yanked back into the brutal reality of the moment by the sharp sting of his palm striking my skin. A sudden, searing heat blooming across my flesh.

Seriously?

"As if that's going to change anything."

Another blow lands, harder this time, the impact stealing my breath. He is not stopping. Are we *really* doing this?

"When I thought you couldn't get any more psychotic, you come up with a punishment straight out of the Dark Ages!"

"Maybe your dear father should have given you a few more when you were young. Might have saved you from being such a fucking pain."

That's it.

"In no fucking world do you get to talk about my father! You know nothing about him—you know nothing about my life!"

I hear him chuckle, low and amused, like my outrage is nothing more than entertainment.

"*Oh*, but I do, Mira. I know everything about you. I know the exact order you eat your breakfast. I know what movies you watch when you're sad, which oat ice cream flavor you reach for when you're happy. I know you secretly dream of living in the world of *Harry Potter* or *Star Wars*, that you have felt misunderstood since the moment you could form a thought, and that the second alcohol touches your lips, you transform into fucking *Céline Dion*. Nothing slips past me. Least of all, *you.*"

Tears slip down my face effortlessly. Sorrow? No, not quite. Sadness? His comment about my father cut deep, but I was not exactly kind either. Fear? No. I have come to understand that fear excites me, that I *need* it to feel truly alive.

It's something else entirely.

Then it hits me—it's *joy.*

Joy that someone sees me, *truly* sees me. That someone knows me in ways I did not even know I wanted to be known. That someone pays attention to the smallest, most insignificant details of my existence. Joy in the way he makes me feel free—paradoxically—even as I am bound to his will. In the way he drags me into experiences I never imagined possible, into a world where I feel *more*.

"Xan... Hit me again."

His body goes rigid behind me, every muscle tensing in an instant. He clearly did not expect that. Hell, *I* did not expect that. Though for once, I silence the voice in my head that tries to analyze, to control every outcome. Instead, I listen to a force deeper, primal which tells me to trust him. To trust that he will know exactly how far to take me—not too much, not too little, just perfectly enough.

A shiver rolls through my chest, spreading like wildfire, leaving a trail of goosebumps in its wake. Sparks crackle beneath my skin, a dizzying rush of electricity coursing through my veins, between my legs and it is exhilarating. Addictive. I want *more*.

I want him to *ruin* me. I want to be shattered, undone, left trembling beneath the supremacy of his touch and the power of his control.

"Are you going to hit me, or should I wait for the corpse to do it for you?"

The first strike lands before I have even finished my sentence. Then another. And another. Each one sharper, each one searing through the flesh like fire licking at bare nerves. My breath hitches, stolen by the vigor of it, by the brutal poetry of pain unraveling across my body.

"Show me," I whisper, trembling but certain. "Show me how wicked I've been. Show me how much you want me to regret walking away from you."

The punishment continues, relentless, merciless. My curves hums with the sensation—sharp, stinging, alive. It takes me a moment to realize that the warmth trickling down my skin is mine, that the crimson staining my body is not his nor from the dead man beside me.

It is me.

My shell breaking beneath the weight of his fury. Even so, I make no move to leave. I want more. I want to be stripped bare under his hands and remade by the violence of his need.

His heartbeat crashes against mine, thundering in the silence, like an impending cyclone ready to destroy everything in its path. Every muscle straining with desire, as if he is teetering on the brink of insanity. His voice, barely more than a rasp, drips with frustration and hunger.

"Be careful what you wish for, Mira," he murmurs, the words coated in dark warning. "You will regret this, just like you regret your actions right now."

I don't care. I feel it now—this deep, burning need that surges through me like a tidal wave. I am lost to it. I need him, I want him, and I know there is no turning back. The ache inside me only intensifies, drowning me, pulling me deeper into a whirlpool of raw, uncontrollable passion.

I hear the sharp sound of his zipper tearing open, his cock finally released, exposed.

"Fuck, you know you're leaving me with no other choice, little fox. If you were not so damn beautiful, so irresistibly hot, and so fucking stubborn, I wouldn't be pushed to do all of this to you."

"Do what needs to be done. Even if it destroys me. I've already made peace with the pain."

I turn to him, desperate to see his face, his reaction. Again, the mask stands between us, an impenetrable wall. That damn mask. The one I had momentarily forgotten in the mayhem of this night. My eyes search for his, though all I can find is darkness. I want to believe he is looking back at me, that he sees me, really sees me.

"Maybe I'm overstepping," I whisper. "But this... whatever this is between us... it cannot truly exist if you keep that barrier forever..."

A silence so dense it threatens to crush the air from my lungs hangs.

"I know."

The heaviness of it crushes me. Not just the words, but the way he says them. Like a man bound by chains he cannot break, no matter how much they cut right into his bones. Maybe he does not want to break them. Maybe he believes he can't. But I feel it. The sorrow just beneath the surface, the war raging inside his heart, the torment of a man who has been trapped for too long. A man who doesn't know what it is like to be free.

I wish I could lift this burden from his shoulders, strip away the weight he carries so relentlessly—but I know he is not ready. And I respect that. What I know, with absolute certainty, is that *I* am ready. Ready to take the last part of my punishment.

I arch my back, pressing myself against his dick, dragging my ass over the hardness that I know is meant for me. An offering. A challenge. A plea. I cannot endure the wait any longer. I am so overwhelmed with desire that merely imagining what he might do to me pushes me to the verge of delirium.

His hand moves swiftly, expecting another sharp strike. To my surprise, it slips between my thighs. Heat floods me instantly as his fingers graze my sensitive nerves, trailing with agonizing slowness until they rest against the aching pulse at my core. The tenderness of his touch is such a stark distinction to the violent strikes that came before, and the sensation is nothing short of intoxicating.

"You're absolutely drenched, Mira," he murmurs, his voice a sinful caress. "Think you could come for me?"

His fingers find their place, gliding over my clit with slow, deliberate circles, the pressure just right—enough to make my eyes roll back.

"Xan... it feels so good."

With Julian, I always ended up reaching for toys, his touch as sensual as a piece of unfinished wood. Nothing like this. Nothing like *him*.

"I asked you a question."

His movements quicken, coaxing pleasure from me so effortlessly it is almost infuriating. He is way too good at this. Too practiced. The realization ignites a brief, ridiculous flicker of jealousy. I know it is absurd, but I cannot help it.

He seizes himself with a firm grip, the hotness of his cock pulsing against his palm, letting it fall in sharp, rhythmic slaps against my ass cheeks. Every strike ignites a fresh wave of sensation, a cruel mix of fire and ecstasy that tightens my throat and steals my breath. My skin, raw and aching, trembles beneath his touch, each impact sending shockwaves through my entire body.

Even the mere brush of air feels excruciating, each live wire alight with overstimulation. A broken moan slips past my lips— part torment, part desperate surrender.

"I fucking asked you a question. I don't think you're in any position to ignore me."

His words slice through the thick, electric tension hanging between us, sharp and unrelenting. There is no room for hesitation, no escape from the dominance in his tone.

Will I surrender? The answer is carved into every aching inch of me. My body trembles with need, my breath shattering into uneven gasps. Yet for some inexplicable reason, I still cannot force the words out. Stubborn pride knots itself around my throat, holding me hostage, even as my lower stomach defies me—pleading, begging for more.

"Make me say it," I exhale, syllables soaked in challenge.

A dark, knowing chuckle rumbles through his chest.

"You won't have to tell me twice."

A second later, his fingers penetrate my pussy with devastating precision, tracing slow, tantalizing movements against the most sensitive part of my vagina. A sharp gasp rips through me as pleasure coils tight, winding across my muscles, spreading like liquid fire.

"Is this what you wanted?"

Thoughts refuse to align, let alone an answer. The pressure builds relentlessly, the line between pleasure and torment blurring until they become the same. I grasp at anything—his arms, his shirt, the sheets—desperate for an anchor as he pulls me deeper into oblivion.

"Say it," he commands, his grip tightening just enough to remind me of exactly where I stand.

"Say that you are going to drench the bed with more than your blood, or I stop."

A strangled moan spills from my lips, my last shred of defiance crumbling to dust. He has shattered me, stripped me bare in ways I never imagined, reduced me to nothing but sensation and hunger.

"Please Xan, never stop or I'll die!"

"Well, fucking say it now, before I'm forced to unearth the words buried so deep inside you myself. And though it may sound enticing, I assure you, it will not be."

Euphoria swells to its peak as his touch deepens, sending waves of burning bliss. I have to say it now—if he stops, I swear I will fall apart from this need ripping me open.

I feel like it's as if, by yielding to his demand, I tear down the last of my defenses—those fragile barriers that once held the possibility of saving me, of helping me break free from this emotional entrapment. Since Julian, fear consumes me; nothing feels authentic anymore, and everything is tainted by creeping doubt.

I will not remain this fragile forever. That is the lie I repeat, again and again—while stuck in a version of myself that refuses to be anything else. The past winds around me like barbed wire, its claws embedded too deep to simply shake off. Every scar, every betrayal, every whispered lie is a thread woven into the fabric of who I am. I have spent my life guarding myself, wrapping layers around my heart, convincing myself that I could survive alone. That I *had* to.

Still, here I am, hovering at the cusp of a perilous abyss, a boundless, uncharted expanse. With *him*.

Never have I felt so close to the precipice, yet so achingly safe. As if he is both the storm and the shelter. It would be a lie—a coward's excuse—to hide behind the wounds Julian left when I am the one silently begging Xan to let me in. To lower his mask. To strip away the last layers between us so that we can be whatever we are destined to become.

"Xan, please... never abandon me."

The words spill out before I can stop them and, instantly, shame tangles itself inside me. I want to snatch them back, pretend they never existed. Although it's impossible. Because they are the truest things I have ever said. I have been abandoned too many times to count. My father was stolen to my youth by death. My mother let herself be swallowed by her demons, too mentally broken to fight for me. And Julian... Julian had been nothing but an illusion, a cruel deception I mistook for love.

I brace myself for silence, for indifference, for some kind of reprimand. Instead, Xan exhales slowly, his grip shifting. He releases himself; his palm drags up the length of my spine, a single stroke that is both grounding and electrifying.

"The ones who left you made the biggest mistake of their miserable lives," he breathes. "And me, little fox? I never make mistakes."

With those words, his clap tightens in my hair, yanking my head with just enough force to steal the air from my lungs. My back arches, pressing me flush against him, the rigid heat of his torso searing into mine. I can feel every tense muscle, every controlled breath, as if he is branding me with his presence alone.

Without warning, his fingers sink so much deeper into my pussy, claiming, until my body has no choice but to surrender.

A sharp, unrestrained cry rips from my throat bear by the aching pleasure that sends waves of electricity between my legs.

"Don't test me again, Mira," he warns. "I'm this close to turning from 'cute asshole' to 'full-on nightmare'. So, you better answer me now. For the last time, are you going to come for me?"

My body trembles, pounds in my ears, my skin burning everywhere he touches. I know—there is no running from this. No hiding from what he has awakened.

A shuddering exhale escapes my lips, the last of my defenses crumbling.

"Not only will I come for you, Xan," I whisper, shaking with devotion, "but I swear, from this moment on, you will be the only one who ever makes me."

My words land in the room, solid and immutable, anchoring us in their gravity. His fingers tighten, his body tenses, and for a moment, there is nothing but silence—charged, blistering, a turmoil about to break.

He strokes himself once more, his movements perfectly synchronized with the rhythm he has set against me. Our breaths tangle, rising and falling in unison, a symphony of need and desperation. He leads, and I follow—because, clearly, he is an exceptional dancer. Though I once thought myself suited only for a slow, measured waltz, it turns out I have a taste for a dance far more reckless. He lowers his hard cock corded with veins to my slit, teasing me with the barest touch.

Is *this* finally it? The moment I have been unknowingly waiting for all along. My restraint shatters, disintegrating beneath the weight of sensation—each one crashing over me, relentless, consuming, impossible to outrun.

I am drenched, my body trembling under the slow, torturous rhythm of his fingers, each stroke igniting a deeper need. The pressure he exerts sends liquid heat pooling between my thighs, my walls clenching around the emptiness, dying to be filled.

"Fuck, Mira, you are soaking for me," he groans, trying to restrain. His tip teases at my entrance, barely there. I whimper, desperate. "It's taking everything I have not to bury myself inside your tight little pussy right now."

I throb with the need to have him fully inside, to feel every inch of Xan's dick stretching and filling me.

"I'm barely holding back from sinking down onto you," I plead, my body already revealing just how badly I crave to be fucked.

He keeps the torture, the head of his cock gliding over my slick skin. His fingers move with a slow rhythm, coaxing, claiming—I cannot take it anymore. By the way his breath falters, ragged and uneven, I know he is just as desperate.

"I'm going to come, Xan. Just for you. Only for you."

He lets go of me just long enough to deliver a few sharp slaps to my already tender ass's flesh. The sensation is a wicked blend of pain and pleasure, my body arches instinctively toward him.

A soft, broken moan slips past my lips, yet I offer no resistance—I take it, take *him*, surrendering to the discipline, to the delicious torment of being his.

"Good girl. You have no fucking idea how proud I am."

At his ultimate words, I feel his hard length glide up my lower back, the end of his cock tapping against me in a teasing rhythm—each contact igniting a deeper ache, a need that coils tight in my core.

"*Now*, Mira." His fingers press into me, demanding. "Soak my hand with your pleasure—*drown* me in it. Show me how fucking badly you want this."

I finally unravel, a cry of sheer ecstasy escaping so intense that I feel a rush of warmth spread across my spine, his cum sliding between my cheeks. The timing is flawless, our pleasure intertwining, a perfect harmony that pulses through us. I release completely, more freely than I ever have before, letting my orgasm consume my entire being.

"Damn little fox, feeling how much you're coming is the highest form of praise you could ever give me."

Honestly, I had never responded like this before. With Julian, it was always about his satisfaction, and the rare moments he bothered to return the favor were nothing short of lackluster. It felt more like a half-hearted attempt, like drunk men at a bar stumbling through a dart game, trying to find the target, but missing every time.

"Let me take care of you now," he whispers, his gentle touch clashes with the bruises he's left behind.

He gathers the semen spread on my back, warm against his fingers, and applies it over my burning butt's flesh with tender, measured strokes. I flinch at first, the sting a sharp reminder, but then—the relief blossoms, enveloping my pain like a soft breeze, pulling into its soothing embrace.

If someone had told me that one day I would lie next to a dead man, surrendering to the hands that had punished me, letting them appease the very wounds they inflicted with them cum, my laughter would have erupted like a geyser with a serious attitude problem. Still, here I am—trapped in the space among pain and comfort, discipline and devotion, shame and something that tastes dangerously like love.

Xan shifts, settling beside me while I agonizingly turn onto my back. His pack of cigarettes rests just within reach, and flicks one out, lighting it with a deep, satisfied sigh.

"As much as I'm enjoying the view you're giving me, it is time you put some clothes on. One of the Order's assistants will be here soon, and trust me, you don't want him to see you naked. I'd rather not have to explain to his boss why he'd need to send another employee to clean up after *two* bodies."

Placing my dress over my stomach, he gestures for me to stand, a silent command I obey without hesitation. With a subtle motion, he directs me to position myself before him. I comply once more, wordless, drawn to the quiet authority in his gaze.

"Far be it from me to suggest that this dress doesn't make you look absolutely mesmerizing," he murmurs, taking a long drag from his cigarette. "But before you dress up, I want to see you—every inch of you."

He looks effortlessly regal, lounging there with that quiet confidence, exuding mystery, a man with the world at his feet. And for reasons beyond my understanding, he has chosen me. He has decided that it is my body he desires, my curves he worships, my red hair, my pale eyes.

The impact of that realization crashes over me. I have never known what it feels like to *really* belong to someone, to be wanted like *this*. With him, I feel it—a tether, an unshakable pull. He proves me that I am not alone in this solitary world. That, for the first time, I have an ally to stand beside. That, for the first time, I can belong to something—someone.

A home.

A *family*.

Chapter 20

XAN

*H*er body is sheer perfection, sculpted as if the gods of beauty themselves had taken their time, carving every dip and curve with divine precision.

I am not a believer—not in gods, not in fate—but right now? I would gladly drop to my knees and worship at the altar of her form without a second thought. If this is blasphemy, then consider me a devoted sinner, because I am absolutely fantasizing about a sacred marble masterpiece, and I have zero regrets.

The fiery copper of her hair glows even in the dim shadows of the room, a beacon against the darkness. However, it is her eyes that hold me captive—pools of quiet suffering, etched with the ghosts of every abandonment she has endured. Yet, beneath the weight of all that pain, there is something new flickering in their depths. A fragile ember of hope, hesitant but undeniable, as if for the first time, she dares to think she is no longer alone.

She would be right to believe it—because the only force that could tear me from her now is death itself. And I don't mean hers. If she were to slip away from this world, I would not stay in it for long. I would follow without hesitation, willingly surrendering to the emptiness just to find her on the other side. Because I realize that a life without her is no life at all, merely an existence—empty, hollow, and devoid of any meaning.

As she finishes dressing, I take one last drag of my cigarette, the ash glowing in the chamber before I turn and crush it out. When I face forward again, my gaze lands on the man who dared to manipulate my girl, who used a masked face to deceive Mira—to violate what is hers alone to give, and mine alone to worship.

"You should have turned your eyes elsewhere," I murmur. "Away from the innocence of my little fox."

I crouch beside him, grasping his lifeless face with cold precision. His vacant, unseeing globes stare up at me as I reach out, pulling down his lower eyelid. With the same ruthless efficiency with which he once hunted his prey, I press the burning ember of my cigarette against the delicate tissue of his retina. The hiss of searing flesh sizzling. Smoke curls. The acrid scent of scorched meat lingers in the air, an offering to the cruelty he inflicted.

Mira watches me, her expression unreadable—curious, disturbed, yet... exhilarated. I know that look. I see the way she is unfolding, shedding the last remnants of the girl she was, stepping fully into the woman she is becoming.

With one hand, I retrieve another cigarette, lighting it slowly, inhaling deeply until the heat sears through my lungs. With the other, I reach for Mira, guiding her into my lap, pulling her against me. I feel her settle, warm and pliant, as the world burns around us. I trace lazy patterns along her thigh as I let her take in the sight before us—the delicate consumption of flesh by flame. It is almost poetic, in its own grotesque way. The irony is not lost on me.

It feels like one of those quiet, intimate moments shared between lovers—like a couple curled up by a crackling campfire, passing a cigarette, lost in the dance of the flames. Except our fire is a man's ruined face, and the only thing we are burning through is the last shred of his existence.

We sit in silence, the only sound the soft inhale and exhale of smoke leaving my lips. The air is thick with the scent of scorched flesh and nicotine, and somehow, this moment feels... peaceful.

"Isn't it nice, little fox?" I say, amusement curling at the edge of my voice. "You and me, wrapped up together by the fire."

She lets out a laugh, light and sharp, smacking my arm.

"You're so stupid."

"I know." I grin, taking another drag. "Now, it's your turn."

I extend the cigarette toward her, positioning it into her trembling hand. She shudders the moment her fingers close around it—a tremor caught in the balance of fear and anticipation, but she still takes it.

"As far as I remember, he looked at you with *both* of his eyes, didn't he?" I say in a smooth, mischievous way. "I command it for me... but in the end, I want it to be for you."

She hesitates, staring down at the still body before her, the cinder flickering between her fingertips, a primal war raging in her mind. I see the moment her resolve falters, her breath hitching as she freezes just before making contact. She needs support. It is natural. It is expected. And I will always be there to give it to her—especially when her first kill will come.

I move to steady her hand, but before I can, she steels her nerves and takes the final step forward. All she needed was the smallest push, a whisper of assurance.

In that moment, with more force than I used—so much more, and hell, that makes my dick going berserk again—she drives the cigarette into the remaining eye. The flesh boiling on impact, the wet crackle of burning tissue filling the hotel room as the heat consumes what is left.

Then... she smiles. A small, wicked thing curling at the edges of her lips.

And *God* help me; she has never looked more beautiful.

Covered in blood, in sweat, in the remnants of her own transformation. She is carved from fire and vengeance, from ashes and untamed, unbreakable force.

She is, without a doubt, the woman of my fucking life.

Chapter 21

XAN

Morning has barely broken, a faint light slipping through the curtains of my room, and already, my mood is as stormy as last night. Mira sleeps in her own room, where I took her after our little escapade. I stayed outside her door for a while, listening to her breathing, making sure she found at least a sliver of peace—one wrapped in ashes and dried blood.

Me, though? I did not sleep. Not really. The adrenaline faded, but the irritation never did. I reach for my phone and dial Lucian, stretching out on my bed as the call rings. When he picks up, I shut him down before he even starts.

"Morning, sunshine," I purr, stretching lazily. "Tell me, how does it feel to be your own financial liability? Paying a man to clean up the corpse of another man you also paid? That's got to sting."

I let a beat of silence hang, just long enough to let the humiliation sink in.

"Personally?" I let out a low chuckle. "I think it is the funniest shit I have ever seen. Almost makes me want to let you keep going just to see what else you will waste your money on."

I exhale slowly, letting the last traces of laughter fade, my tone shifting with it. Because as much as I enjoy getting under his skin, this is not why I called.

"Listen, Mira is going to rise in this world, whether is with or without you. She has the drive. And the smarts. What is coming next for her—it's not even a choice. It is inevitable. And I will gladly be the one who shapes it."

I hear the restraint in his breath, the tension behind his silence—but this? This part is out of his hands.

Because my little fox and I? We are fucking unstoppable. And now that she wants me by her side, no one will touch us.

"Mira's completely blind to the truth about her father." I continue. "She has no clue what she is capable of, though I saw it in her yesterday. And that kind of skill? Practically extinct"

I pause, my tone deepening as the meaning of the words settles in.

"You and I have been at each other's throats for too long now. It is time we stop tearing ourselves down and start looking at what is right in front of us. We can have Mira on our side, and she'll never need to know the truth about Edmond. I'll make sure of that. She can't ever find out I was there when it all happened."

The thought alone sends a bullet through my chest.

"Do you understand what I'm saying, Lucian? This is not just about the Order. It's about *her*. Her past is irrelevant. She will become exactly what I mold her to be. We do this my way, or I'll burn the Order into the fucking ground with you on top of it."

Lucian stays silent; however I know he's dissecting my words, breaking them down the way he always does. I push myself up, pacing slowly across the room, the phone still to my ear.

"Let's stop wasting time," I press on. "You and I both know where this is headed. Mira belongs in the Order. She always has. She has already proven that. So, will you take my offer, or shall we keep playing this game of cat and mouse—both of us fully aware that we are far too skilled to ever truly lose?"

I hear through the phone a small noise—a growl, a delightful mix of frustration and a sigh.

"I want her to have at least one kill under her belt before we officially bring her in," finally says Lucian. "And don't tell her about the Order's intentions—just find her a target and evaluate her performances."

A low chuckle escapes me, a knowing smirk forming. I already have a clear direction in mind.

"You'll hear from me soon enough," I retort, ending the call.

Now that this is settled, Mira can finally return home. But there is not a chance in hell I will let her out of my sight—not even for a second. She is far too precious to me and, from this moment on, to the Order as well.

I knock twice on her door. Not hard. Just to let her know I mean business, but not enough to wake the dead. Mira, however, groans like I have just triggered the apocalypse.

"Rise and shine, Ginger," I lean against the wall. "You've got ten seconds before I break this door down and carry you out wrapped in your sheets like some kind of gothic breakfast burrito."

Silence.

I smirk. I know this game.

"Ten. Nine. Eight—"

The door swings open mid-countdown, and I am greeted by a very grumpy, sleep-drunk Mira, her hair a chaotic mess, one of my black shirts slipping off her shoulder.

"*You,*" she rasps, voice still asleep, "are the worst part of my morning."

"Still," I drawl, tilting my head, "you opened the door."

"Because you count like a fucking psychopath."

"I *am* a psychopath." I grin under the mask. "Now, come on. You have earned a croissant. Or ten. I'm not one to comment."

She sighs so hard you would think I just asked her to walk to Paris to get it. She flips me off and disappears back inside to get dressed.

Fifteen minutes later, we are tucked into a secluded corner of the hotel café. The scent of coffee lingers in the air like a warm fog, thick and rich. Mira stirs her oat milk latte absentmindedly, staring at it like it might betray her.

Across from her, I pull up my mask just enough to sip my black coffee—because anything else is blasphemy in my honest opinion—and watch her with an amused tilt of my head.

"You know," I muse, "for someone who fought like a wild animal last night, you are very delicate with that spoon."

Mira eyes me over her coffee cup, disbelief written all over her face.

"You are seriously judging me while sitting in a café, at 7 a.m., wearing a full-on horror movie mask? People are staring, Xan."

I shrug, utterly unbothered. "Let them. Maybe they think I'm a celebrity."

"Or a serial killer."

I place a hand over my heart, feigning deep offense.

"Wow. Hurtful."

She rolls her eyes, but I see it—the way she swallows back a laugh like it physically pains her. She will not give me the satisfaction. Not yet. But I will get it out of her. I always do.

She glares at me over the rim of her mug.

"God, just let me wake up."

"So dramatic." I take another slow sip. "Do you need me to feed you? Cut your croissant into tiny little pieces? Maybe airplane the fork into your mouth?"

"I need you to shut the hell up."

"That's never going to happen."

She sighs once more, but I catch the twitch of her lips—she is fighting it. "You are insufferable."

"And yet," I lean forward, resting my elbow on the table, "here you are, having breakfast with me. *Again.*"

She does not answer right away, just breaks off a piece of her pastry and pops it into her mouth. I wait.

"Stockholm Syndrome," she finally mutters.

I chuckle, shaking my head. "Not *yet*, little fox. But soon."

Chapter 22

MIRA

I'm lost in the haze of my thoughts, considering the next steps are tangled in the aftermath of everything. The hotel room, the dangerous tension, the whispers of power. But there is something else I need to handle.

"I must call Zoey... and my work. They are going to freak out if they don't hear from me soon." Xan's gaze sharpens.

"You're not going to just disappear, are you?", he says, teasing, but there's an edge, a reminder of who he is. A predator. And I'm still his prey. I know he watches me with that unsettling intensity.

I roll my eyes. "Of course not. They might think I'm dead. I just..." I pause, trying to gather my feelings, but they feel scattered. "I need to clear things up with them. Especially with Zoey. She must be worried sick."

I glance at him, unsure of how he will react. He says nothing for a long moment, then, with a slight shrug, he speaks again, his tone a mix of exasperation and amusement.

"And what exactly are you going to tell her? 'Oh, sorry, I was just kidnapped by some dangerous guy, huge cock though, but hey, let's get a drink tomorrow.'"

I cannot help the laugh that bubbles up from my chest. It is bitter, laced with the tension I am still fighting to push down.

"Something like that, yeah."

Xan leans back, his eyes scanning me as if he is weighing the consequences of this conversation.

"Just make sure she doesn't ask too many questions. We do not need anyone poking around and getting too curious."

I nod, feeling a pang of guilt for dragging Zoey into this mess. But she is my best friend. I cannot just cut her out, not completely at least.

"How about the apartment?" Xan asks with concern. Or maybe it is just the usual control he so effortlessly wields. "Are you going to go back there?"

I hesitate. The thought of Julian's things, the mess of him that still clings to that place feels like a burden on my chest.

"Yeah. I need to get his stuff out. I can't have his ghost haunting in the background, not when... everything is changing."

I meet his eyes for a moment, challenging him to question it. Xan's smirk is back, that dark, confident expression I have come to expect from him even through his mask.

"You want me to come with you? Make sure things don't get... complicated?"

I raise an eyebrow at him, fighting the smile that wants to creep up.

"You mean you want to come for the fun of it, don't you?"

He shrugs, unbothered.

"It's not every day I get to watch you clean up after your little shitty ex. I'd call it a sport if I wasn't already busy with more important things."

I roll my eyes, but cannot help the amusement that flickers in me.

"*Fine.* But you will have to stay still while I actually do the cleaning. No way I'm letting you touch anything. Especially not his stuff."

Xan leans forward, suddenly quieter, more serious.

"You're not really going to let her in on all this, *are you?* Zoey, I mean. It's too much. If she finds out the truth... well, let's just say we don't need to add another loose end to tie up."

I feel a flash of anger.

"She's my best friend, Xan. Ignoring her is not an option."

"I'm not saying you should. But you need to keep a tight grip on what you tell her. Things are already fucked enough."

I look at him, frustration rising.

"I know what I'm doing, Xan. I'm not some naïve idiot."

He leans back again, watching me like he's waiting for me to crack. "We'll see," he mutters, the sharpness in his gaze never leaving mine.

How fucking dare he?

"I swear to God, Xan—*try me.* I am not in the mood to be disrespected, not by you, not by anyone," I respond with fury—barely leashed, seconds from snapping.

I am not stupid, geez. I am fully aware I cannot let a soul know too much.

"Alright," I finally say, standing up and pulling my coat tighter around me. "I'll call Zoey and I will get this done. But I'm not doing it alone." I look at Xan. "So, you can either stay out of the way or come along for the ride. I don't care."

He smirks, clearly enjoying this. "You'll have to take me along then. Would not miss it for the world. Can't wait to piss on his pillow."

I roll my eyes, though part of me braces—because I know he's joking. At least, I hope he is. Xan rises too, stretching his arms high above his head—damn it, I catch myself admiring all the way down to the sharp V of his lower abdomen disappearing beneath his waistband.

Despite the attitude problem, the god complex, and the overall infuriating aura, he somehow manages to redirect my focus to his redeeming qualities... like being a fiercely protective menace and a walking, talking, brooding human red flag with muscles.

"Careful, soon I'll have to call you *little Saint Bernard*."

I narrow my eyes, completely baffled. What the hell is he talking about now?

"You're drooling all over the place."

I cannot even respond, he is driving me crazy—though I cannot decide if it is because he has nailed me so perfectly, or because he is just utterly ridiculous.

I turn to continue walking. Before I can even process what is happening, he slaps my ass with a laugh that is so effortlessly carefree, so damn normal. Like we are not two people caught in a chaotic mess, but a couple heading out for a peaceful walk to pick up our two kids from school, hand in hand, strolling back to our cute cottage tucked away from this fucked up world.

The ease with which he does it catches me off guard completely. For a split second, my brain goes blank. I am unsure how to respond. Still, as farfetched as it sounds, that fleeting image of quiet domesticity does not feel entirely unwelcome.

———— 🐾 ————

While Xan is driving the stolen car from the gala, I pause to send Zoey a message telling her to meet me at the apartment. Giving that she is on her day off, and that she never lets the first day of break slip by without indulging in complete idleness, I am not even the slightest bit worried. I know she will drop everything and rush to me, no questions asked, like she always does when I need her.

> First of all, I'm sooo sorry for disappearing, and second, could you come at my apartment, like now? 😢 😢 😢

As I expected, her reaction is anything but calm, and I cannot say I blame her.

> I CAN'T BELIEVE YOU DID THIS TO ME, YOUR GODDAMN BFF !!! 😠 😠 😱

I know, I know. This is not exactly how you win *Best Friend of the Year*, but choice has not exactly been on the menu lately.

> I'll explain everything at the apartment. Just please, come meet me. I need you.

Seconds drag by in silence, each one heavier than the last, until my phone finally buzzes in my hand.

> Fine. Oh, and just so you know, I hate you. 🖤

With that one reply, I already miss her endlessly. It is ridiculous how fast the ache settles in—and of course, as if Xan's suddenly fluent in my inner monologue...

"You will see her soon, pull yourself together, girl. Any more of this and I might get jealous."

I elbow him in the arm, half playful, half warning. I know damn well how hard he is working right now—against every one of his instincts and twisted principles—to let me go see Zoey. Even more so to let me *introduce* him to her, still searching for the right words to say.

When we finally arrive at the apartment, a knot twists tighter in my chest, and whether it is thrill or dread—I cannot even tell anymore. Xan parks the car smoothly, but I can feel the tension. He follows me inside, his presence as solid and unyielding as always, yet his silence makes me wonder what's going on in his mind.

Zoey is already there. *Of course she is.* I forgot she has the damn key. As I step inside, the familiar scent of her perfume hits me first—the faint trace of lavender and something warm, like coffee on a lazy Sunday morning. Zoey's lounging on the couch, her feet tucked under her, phone in hand, looking as if she had been waiting for hours instead of just a few minutes.

She looks up when I walk in; her face lighting up with that familiar, mischievous grin that always makes me feel like I have just been caught doing something I should not.

"Mira!" she cries out, her voice full of relief. Her arms fly open as though I am the most long-lost treasure in the world. "Finally! I thought you'd gotten abducted by aliens or *worse*—kidnapped by that weird freak from the bar!"

I laugh, rolling my eyes at her teasing, yet that sense of relief is shortlived. The moment she looks past me and locks eyes with Xan, the world shifts as if someone suddenly hit pause on everything.

She freezes. The bright, carefree expression she had when she first saw me instantly disappears. Her eyes sweep over Xan, and just like that, it clicks—sharp, wary, alert.

"Oh, *hell* to the no!"

I can see the exact moment when Zoey's brain short-circuits. Her eyes widen, her shoulders tense, and for a split second, I think she might just turn around and run. She is trying to process him, to figure out if I have just brought a professional villain into our life. Based on the look on her face, she is already forming a thousand theories about who he could possibly be. Her lips remain sealed for a moment, just stares, her mouth parted in disbelief. I can feel the awkwardness making me want to dig a hole and crawl into it.

Zoey shakes her head to clear the fog in her brain and finally finds her voice.

"Mira, what the actual fuck is going on? Is he... is he... like the Grim Reaper?"

She points a shaky finger toward Xan, her tone rising in pitch.

"I swear, he looks like he's about to drag me to the underworld!"

I cringe, but somehow still funny. Zoey has that look on her face—the one that says she is equal parts terrified and oddly fascinated.

No doubt about it—Xan does feel like he stepped out of some dark, twisted fairy tale. The black clothes. The mask. The entire aura of someone who should be in a *Scream* movie.

I quickly step forward, trying to salvage this before she spontaneously combusts.

"Zoey, this is Xan," I say, rushing out a little too quickly. "He's... kind of important to everything that has been going on. Trust me, I did not just pick him up off the street."

Zoey's eyes widen even more.

"Well, *thank God* for that, because this guy? He looks like he'd steal my soul and still expect a tip!"

I hear a small chuckle from Xan. Sadly, the weight in the room remains untouched. Zoey takes a step back, her hand instinctively reaching for the nearest weapon—her phone.

"Please tell me you're not about to take me to some underground lair and make me join your evil army?" she asks sarcastically.

Xan stays perfectly still, not a single twitch. He just stands there, all mysterious and Zoey's defenses cranking up to full blast now. I swear, her instincts are sharper than a cat on a hot tin roof. I rub my temples, already exhausted.

"Zoey, please, it's not what you think..."

Zoey is not done. She now circles Xan, studying him the way one studies a puzzle, determined to solve it.

"No, no, *no*," she mutters to herself. "You can't just walk in here wearing that mask and expect me to be okay with it. Seriously, what do you do? Rip hearts out for a living?"

Xan, still silent, just raises an eyebrow beneath the mask from the look of his gaze, and I can almost hear his internal monologue.

Yes, absolutely.

Zoey finally turns back to me, her eyes narrowed.

"You seriously brought this... guy... here, *huh*? The sicko that almost killed a man at the bar in front of everybody, lurking in the shadows, just waiting for me to hand over my firstborn?" I throw my hands up.

"Oh my God, I promise, he's not here to steal your firstborn nor the second! But I really need you to just—"

Zoey interrupts dramatically and clearly exaggerating.

"Ah, I get it now. You're just keeping me around for when things really go south, *huh*? I'm your emergency contact for the apocalypse." I groan, facepalming.

"Zoey, we are not at the end of the world. Please, just..."

Zoey turns back to Xan, hands on her hips, giving him a once-over.

"Okay, then," she says, suddenly upbeat, almost too cheery. "If you're not here to eat my soul with fucking ketchup, I'm guessing I'm supposed to be impressed? Because right now, I'm just terrified and slightly underwhelmed."

Zoey might be freaking out, but at least she is still Zoey—sassy, sarcastic, and a bit too dramatic for her own good.

"Listen, I know you are probably going to hate me for what I'm about to say, but I can't exactly explain the *why* of Xan. There is so much more to it, things I cannot even begin to put into words. What you need to understand is *this*—he is the reason I'm still here, still breathing I mean. Without him, I wouldn't be alive to stand in front of you."

I turn my head slowly, locking eyes with Xan, who is already watching me with an intensity that makes my breath hitch. His gaze holds a thousand unspoken words, so much meaning conveyed in the silent connection we share. I offer him a small, almost imperceptible nod, a silent gesture of gratitude, hoping that it speaks volumes in return.

His hand moves, a soft touch against the small of my back—nothing more than a brief caress. Still, it feels like a promise, a vow.

You are the war I would die for, little fox.

The simple movement sends a surge of heat through me, a jolt that makes my heart skip a beat. I can feel the weight of his touch, even after it's gone. My body reacts before my mind can catch up, a shiver running down my spine that I fight to conceal. Every part of me wants to hide the effect he is having on me, especially in front of Zoey, but it is impossible. Even the smallest gestures from him is enough to leave me undone, to make my pulse race and my mind spin.

And Xan... he knows it. He is fully aware of the way he makes me lose control, of how even the slightest touch can send me into a frenzy. The satisfaction in his eyes is unmistakable. He revels in it; in the power he has over me. For some inexplicable reason, I cannot bring myself to care. I am tangled in it—him, the chaos, the danger.

Zoey watches me closely, her gaze sharp. She is searching for any cracks, any sign that I might hide something more than I am letting on, looking for the truth behind the words, the hidden layers I have not dared to speak.

I remain still, my expression guarded, revealing nothing but the absolute honesty of what I have just told her. The truth about Xan, about how he saved me—*that* much is real, and I won't let her see anything else. The past is a murky pool, one I am not ready to dive into, not yet.

Thought I can feel her digging, probing, looking for something more, I keep it locked inside. The only thing she's allowed to know is the sincerity of what I have said—the simple, visceral truth that Xan is the reason I still exist in this world.

My attention snaps away, drawn unwillingly to the mess of Julian's things scattered across the room—the man who betrayed me for a damn promotion. This mess is rotting me from the inside. I must erase it.

"I'm sorry. I wish I could give you more details, but I've got to get rid of Julian's stuff, and I need to do it now."

Zoey raises an eyebrow, her curiosity piqued.

"Funny you mention that. I was about to ask what happened to him. Not that I was ever a fan of his pathetic excuse for a person. Although, changing men like socks is not exactly your thing, *is it?*"

Before I can respond, Xan's voice cuts in, smooth and self-assured.

"How could she resist my irresistible charm?" Zoey laughs, the sound playful, but biting.

"Oh, trust me, you need more than charm. I mean, who knows? Maybe under that ridiculous mask of yours, you're hiding a face full of bloody pimples and a bleached monobrow."

Xan steps forward, closing the distance between them, his presence suddenly overwhelming. He leans in, his voice dropping to a dangerous whisper that makes the room feel smaller.

"Let me make something clear, dear Zoey," he says, darkly amused. "My charm is the *least* of it. Without showing my face, without a single kiss, without even riding her sweet tight pussy with my imposing dick, I've managed to make your best friend come so fucking hard to the point where she wouldn't care if I was Quasimodo himself."

Zoey's eyes widen, her mouth opening and closing like a fish out of water. Meanwhile, I try to hide the mix of horror and laughter threatening to bubble up inside me. This is Xan—irresistible, infuriating, and completely *ridiculous* in the most unexpected way.

I let them battle it out, each trying to out-stubborn the other, a silent competition to see which of the two most bullheaded people on the planet would be the first to break. But getting lost in it is not an option—Julian's things are already choking the air out of me.

I start gathering the remnants of the man who once made me believe I mattered, who convinced me I was important in his heart, only to leave me drowning in the aftermath of his disgusting lies.

Each object I touch feels is a cruel reminder, a sharp stab of betrayal. His belonging—his presence—I need them gone, erased, as though I realize they were never part of my life to begin with.

After a few hours, there is barely a trace of him left. The atmosphere feels lighter, as if the walls themselves are relieved to be rid of his shadow. Several garbage bags sit by the door, waiting to be sent off to charity. Ironic really, considering the man they once belonged to had never known the meaning of the word.

It stings, just a little, to think that someone out there might one day wear the same shirt as that coward, unknowingly draped in the ghost of my regret. But I have wasted enough years on him—I will not let perfectly good things go to waste too. Let someone else give them a new story.

His chapter here is done.

Chapter 23

MIRA

I sink into the couch beside Zoey and let my head drop onto her shoulder, the weightless surrender that only a best friend can catch. Across the room, Xan leans against the doorway like he's carved into it—watchful, unreadable, carrying that ever-present air of quiet torment. There is a softness to his look now, a rare flicker of contentment at seeing me breathe easier beside a friend who knows the real me.

Zoey gently strokes my hair, the way she used to when we were teenagers hiding from the world. We both stare down at the garbage bags near the door as if they were cursed relics.

"You have to tell me what happened, Mira. I mean... you loved Julian," she says softly.

Xan's entire body shifts—subtle, but seismic. His arms tighten; his shoulders lift slightly. *Jealousy.* Not the loud, messy kind. His is quiet. Lethal.

Because even if she was only speaking in past tense, even if Julian is just trash waiting to be hauled out, the idea that I ever loved someone else—that someone else touched the parts of me Xan now holds like sacred fire—is enough to make him burn.

And honestly? I could get used to it.

"I don't really want to talk about it... Let's just say that, once again, if it hadn't been for Xan, I would probably still be stuck under the sweaty arms of some greasy old pervert."

Zoey stays quiet for a moment. I can see her brain working, trying to stitch meaning from the scraps I am telling her.

I cannot blame her. I have given her so little to hold on to, and yet she is still here, persevering.

After a brief pause, she lifts one brow and says, with a crooked little smile.

"Was he rich at least?"

The laughter bursts out of me like a pressure valve cracking open—sharp, loud, and so desperately needed. She joins me, our voices climbing over one another like they used to when we were fifteen and fearless.

"Yeah," I say through giggles, wiping a tear from my cheek. "But he definitely had a tragically tiny dick."

We both fall into hysterics, the kind that steals your breath and makes your ribs ache. For a second, the world tilts back into a place that feels like home. Even Xan cannot help but chuckle—whether it is at our absurd jokes or just at us. Either way, the moment feels warm and right, a balm over bruised skin. He steps forward and gently takes my hand in his.

"Alright, ladies," he says, low but amused, "I will handle the charity bags. You two deserve a drink—hell, maybe five. Grab a cab, go sip something sinful, and if you're not stumbling back with mascara tears and inside jokes that make no sense, you're doing it wrong."

I glance down. My palm is now filled with twenties—crisp, clean, and far too many.

"I can pay for my own things, you know," I protest, lifting my eyes to meet his.

Except Zoey is quicker. She snatches the bills with the speed of a woman possessed.

"Geez, are you insane? You say thank you and run before he changes his mind. Go, go, GO!"

She grabs her purse and yanks me by the arm with the force of a tornado in heels. My feet barely brush the ground as she drags me toward the door. I twist back to catch a sight of Xan, smiling at him through the whirl of motion. He meets my gaze with a knowing wink before gently closing behind us.

Let's be real—a tiny part of me expects to come back to a ceremonial bonfire of Julian's belongings blazing in the middle of my living room. I remind myself: *trust.* I need to let him in. Even if he has an unhinged glint in his eye when it comes to my ex.

After several hours of laughter, whispers, and just enough poor decisions to call it a proper night, Zoey—true to her form—had indulged in a few more drinks than me. Especially knowing it was all on Xan's tab. I, ever the slightly more responsible one, stuck to three delicate flutes of sparkling wine. Just enough to hush the swirl of emotions inside me, but not enough to drown them completely.

As Zoey swayed off toward her apartment with a slurred *"text me when you get laid,"* I sent her home to sleep off the three—or maybe six—extra glasses she definitely did not need.

Maybe it's the wine. Maybe it's the weight of the day finally peeling off my chest—but as I step out of the cab and climb the stairs, I feel a curious flutter of excitement at the thought of finding Xan waiting for me.

Could we ever live a life like this? The kind where you unlock the door, toss your keys in a bowl, and call out, *'Honey, I'm home!'* without irony or bloodstains?

I turn the knob slowly, half-expecting something to leap out at me—like a dramatic squirrel with a vendetta or Xan holding a flamethrower made of Julian's underwear. What I find instead still knocks the breath out of me.

An aisle of rose petals. Crimson, fragrant, some absurd scene from a romance film we would both laugh at in any other context.

I blink.

Once.

Twice.

Then smile.

Of course.

Leave it to the emotionally constipated assassin to turn my apartment into a florist's fever dream.

I tiptoe forward, heart fluttering with a ridiculous mix of excitement and suspense, ready to find Xan sprawled across the bed like some vintage romance novel cover—shirtless, draped in a bear faux fur with a glass of whiskey and a fireplace roaring behind him.

As I follow the trail of rose petals deeper into the apartment, an eerie sound reaches my ears—a soft, muffled squeak. Curious and somewhat alarmed, I creep toward the bedroom door, which hangs slightly ajar. Candlelight spills out in flickering waves, casting mystical golden shadows into the hallway.

I push the door open with a mix of caution and anticipation, my breath stopping the second I lay eyes on Xan—bare chest rising and falling with the lazy rhythm of a man who knows he has already won. His skin catches the candlelight, every line of him impossibly perfect and infuriatingly calm, his infamous mask still in place.

I actually find myself enjoying it tonight. There is something maddeningly hot about the mystery. He will take it off when he is ready... although I am aching for that moment more than I would like to admit.

"Well, hello, stranger," I purr, voice dipped in velvet and champagne.

He offers no reply. Just lifts his chin slightly, eyes glinting through the mask, and jerks his head toward the far side of the room. I follow his gaze.

That's when I see it—when I see *him*.

Julian. There. Tied to one of my kitchen chairs as some grotesque display, his mouth sealed shut with layers of duct tape, his panicked little whimpers now making perfect, nauseating sense. He is shirtless, already bleeding—thin slices carved into his shoulders like cruel invitations. But it is the message scrawled in blood across his abdomen that steals my breath.

#2

At first, I fail to understand. The number stares back at me, until finally, I see it—the absurd little gift bow perched on top of his head like a final insult. And suddenly, it clicks.

This is the second gift.

The first was the eye of the man who attacked me at the gala, wrapped up like some gruesome token of devotion. And now *this*—Julian, the man who sold me off without a flicker of guilt, bound and trembling, offered like a sacrifice on a silver altar.

This is Xan's idea of justice. Of romance. Of love.

And I have never felt so truly touched.

222

I turn slowly, pulse still fluttering, only to find Xan already beside me—silent, a shadow summoned by vengeance itself. He offers no words, just lifts his arm and presents a knife I have never seen before.

The blade catches the dim candlelight like a shard of starlight—sleek, retractable, lethally elegant. Along its edge lies an inscription carved deep into the steel.

To Serve the Unseen.

The hilt is obsidian-dark, cool against my skin, crowned with a goldetched emblem I recognize instantly—the Order's seal; a T encircled in ritualistic precision. The moment I wrap my hand around it, a tremor of power coils through me.

A knowing. A claiming.

Like a veil has been lifted.

Like every scar etched into my spirit is sharpening into armor.

With this weapon, I am no longer a prey.

I am the reckoning. I am the finality. I am the answer to every man who has ever mistaken my body for a battlefield.

"Just for you," Xan murmurs softly into my ear, his fingers threading through my hair, the touch gentle yet possessive as he inhales deeply its scent.

Normally, I might have flinched, found the gesture unsettling, too intimate, too strange. But in this world we've woven, where the lines between tenderness and dominance blur, it is nothing but natural. His presence, a dark pull I cannot escape, seems to demand this closeness, this connection.

His hands slide across my body, each movement slow and deliberate, as I stand there, poised, staring down at Julian who's sobbing so loudly I am pretty sure he is auditioning for the role of a gender-switch *Moaning Myrtle*. His tears are pouring so hard, it's like he is trying to drown us all in his own fucking guilt—I'm half-expecting a lifeguard to show up and throw him a pity float.

"Stare into his eyes, Mira. Show him the woman you have become, and the one you're about to be. A power is flowing through you—prove to him he was wrong, that the greatest mistake of his life, his *last* mistake, was underestimating you."

I can feel it now, a strength building inside me, a kind of cold resolve. The absurdity of it all strikes me—there he is, breaking down, while I am standing tall, embracing this twisted evolution of myself, ready to turn the page.

He moves in behind me with a dark, simmering grace, his chest pressing strongly to my back as one hand curls around my breast. His thumb kneads small, delicate circles around my nipple. It is not just a touch; it is a quiet claim, a way of saying *I'm here, and I'm not letting go.* The other slips around to guide mine, his touch patient, possessive, and maddeningly skilled. Our fingers wrap together over the cool handle of the knife, and the weight of it in my palm suddenly feels electric. His breath skims my neck, warm, a lover whispering sins instead of sweet nothings.

224

Slowly, almost reverently, he leads it forward until the cold steel brushes Julian's cheek. A teasing caress at first. Then again—this time in reverse. However, the second stroke is no longer gentle. The edge bites through his skin, enough for blood to bead and trickle down his neck.

At the sight of the cut we've just inflicted, my body arches instinctively, spine curving as my lower back presses against Xan's already hard cock behind me—a desperate plea for grounding, for connection. A breath slips from my lips, rich with unholy satisfaction—unspoken, but screaming with desire.

I take firmer control of the blade, dragging it from the curve of Julian's neck down to the center of his abdomen. The pressure is intentional—enough to make him flinch, enough to remind him he no longer owns me. When I reach the ridges of his stomach, I angle the knife, pressing deeper, testing the resistance of flesh that once thought itself impenetrable.

Behind me, I hear the soft rasp of a zipper being undone, the quiet unveiling of a desire that has been caged far too long. Xan frees himself, thick with anticipation, his breath brushing my shoulder. A bomb waiting to explode.

"God, Mira... you're fucking unbelievable. I have seen nothing more devastatingly beautiful than you wielding that blade like it was born from your very bones."

A twisted sort of pride coats his words.

"I have seen beauty before, but this... this is power. It's pure. It's real. And it's all you, my little fox."

A heat rushes through me at his words, curling around and tightening low in my belly. I have never felt so seen, so desired for the parts of me that were always quiet. My fingers tighten on the handle of the knife with hunger. I turn my head just slightly, a smirk pulling my lips.

"I'm an artist, Xan. You should know that by now—after all that time you spent watching me in the gallery."

He leans in, whispering against the shell of my ear.

"I wasn't just watching, I was studying. Every brushstroke, every line you drew... they told me a story. But nothing compares to what you are painting right now."

His hand tightens ever so slightly on my waist, grounding me.

"This is your masterpiece, Mira. Every mark will be yours to create. His blood will be your paint, and his screams your symphony. You are the artist, and he will be nothing but your darkest realization."

I kneel in front of Julian like I'm about to give a prayer, except this time, the offering is pain. I tap the blade against his thigh while he's trembling, sweat soaking through what is left of his shirt, eyes wide and whimpering like a gutted animal.

Pathetic.

"You used to run your damn mouth non-stop, *remember?* All that confidence, all those empty promises. Where's that big talk now?" I smirk. "Oh right. Buried under the duct tape and the desperation."

He tries to shift, but the ropes bite into him. His chair creaks, feet scraping the floor in useless protest.

I sigh dramatically. "You're twitching like a damn dying fish. Honestly Julian, it's rude. This is supposed to be my special moment."

With no more thinking, I stab the knife clean into the thick of his thigh. Not just a prick—no, I twist it in like I am carving my initials into a tree trunk. He lets out a choked scream under the tape, his eyes rolling, body convulsing in sheer panic.

"There. See?" I say, twisting once more for good measure. "*Now* you're paying me attention."

Blood pours from the wound, spreading across his jeans as I wipe my blade on his collar and rise to my feet slowly.

I glance back at Xan, giving him a sweet, almost innocent smile.

"He twitched too much, baby. Look, I fixed it."

Did I just call him baby?

Maybe it is the alcohol loosening the last threads of inhibition, though for once, I feel I am finally slipping into the skin I was always meant to wear—one that is in control, no longer begging for permission to exist.

The urge to hit him spirals into something feral. My palm lands again and again, until his cheek splits and blood splatters ink across my fingers. The sound—wet, savage echoes, a violent hymn that drowns out the past and baptizes me into the destiny I am about to fulfill.

Before I can even finish, Xan spins me around to face him, my back now shielding me from Julian's pitiful sobs. In one swift motion, he strips off my shirt and bra, exposing me to the candlelit air. The tension in the room thickens as his hands roam my body with purpose. There is an edge to his touch, almost as if he is holding back, yet I can feel the primal need coursing through him. He leans in closer, and I brace myself for what's next.

Instead of diving into the depths of his hunger, he pauses, a flicker in his gaze. With a swift motion, he lifts his mask—just enough to expose his mouth.

His lips graze my stomach gently. The rest of his face stays hidden, still that moment of intimacy feels louder than everything else, more significant than I ever expected. The sensation of his mouth on my skin makes my thighs shake as if they were getting their own earthquake.

His tongue ravages my breast, kissing, biting, worshiping—he is starving and I am the only thing that can feed him.

Xan's teeth scrape across my breast as he drags his mouth lower, nipping, tasting, branding every inch he claims. His hands slide up my ribs, fingers spread wide, trying to memorize the shape of me by touch alone. I arch into him, my breath ragged, my skin burning with the need to be devoured.

"I could carve you into memory," he growls against my flesh, voice gravel and sin. "Every breath you take, every sound you make—it belongs to me now."

The chair creaks again. A whine. Julian's presence, so deplorable, so weak, only heightens the charge in the room. I realize that his despair, that miserable noise of justice finally served, only fuels the ache coiling in me, intensifying the craving I feel for Xan.

I cannot tear my eyes from his mouth—now fully revealed for the first time, far more dangerous than I ever imagined. His lips are thick, sculpted, and unapologetically dominant. They were crafted to command, consume and move with a quiet confidence that makes me more excited than ever. My own lips part of their own accord, trembling in invitation, desperate to be met. When his tongue touches my skin—it is fire meeting silk. My nerves ignite in cascading waves, my body hyperaware, honoring the sensation.

Xan's hand glides along my thigh, unhurried. He moves to my entrance with a devotion that borders on obsession—committing the texture, the warmth, the very essence of me. His fingers press into the deep tender of my vagina, as if imprinting his presence beneath the surface of my body was not enough. Each inch of my pussy he claims sends an electrifying thrill unraveling into my core, a whisper that deepens with every breath.

"I noticed your lips parting," he murmurs, his voice a low velvet drawl that drips with suggestion. "Figured you might search for something to savor."

He wastes no time, bringing his fingers to my mouth—slick with the heat of what he has taken from me, glistening with that indecent, creamy flavor of my surrender. He brushes them over my lower lip first, teasing, observing with sharp eyes as I open wider, soft and wanting. When he finally pushes them in, the taste hits like a jolt—natural, intimate, undeniably mine. He devours me with eyes ablaze, torn between sacred awe and aching desire.

"What you are tasting Mira, is your own liberation. This is the flavor of control, little fox—the kind that only those who dare to surrender can truly understand."

I never thought I could feel this strong in a moment of pure domination. I used to believe that women who submitted were weak, fragile, stripped of any artifice. Yet standing beside the right dominant, I realize how wrong I was.

With Julian, I felt small, suffocated by his attempts to control me. His dominance was a false mask, a lame attempt to keep me beneath him, but it only made me feel incapable, a shadow of myself.

Now, with Xan, I see the difference. It is not about being weak; it is about the strength that rises when you are truly seen, when you are pushed to your limits not by someone's insecurity, but by their power. Julian's dominance only crushed me. This... this makes me whole. *He* makes me whole.

As I savor every lingering trace on his finger, I thrust my fingers deep into my core; the sensation inundating. Xan lets out a satisfied sigh, his breath mingling with the involuntary cry that I let escape. It is as though time halts, the room hums with an electric tension, as euphoria blends with a creeping sense of doom.

"I deemed it necessary for you to experience it—so that you, too, could fully taste the force of my transformation," I whisper as my fingers slip on his tongue, the warmth of my inside wrapping around it.

"Mira, by doing this, you are unlocking a ferocity within me I'm uncertain your body is prepared to withstand."

I chuckle softly, the corners of my lips curling mischievously.

"Xan Hayes, are you actually asking for permission?"

His laughter bursts out, richer than mine, as he responds with a grin.

"As if I'd ever be that foolish."

He lifts me effortlessly, his grip tightening around my waist as he pulls my legs apart, spreading them wide with a feral intensity. My body sinks into his as he moves us towards the bed, the roughness of his touch igniting every nerve.

With one swift motion, he presses me down into the soft sheets, his chest against mine grounding me while his hands roam, owning every part of me. My legs, now sprawled on either side, feel the heat of his hands as he positions me with ruthless force, ordering me to feel the full intensity of his desire.

"But before I allow you to taste the overwhelming power of what I carry, I must finish the feast you so graciously invited me to enjoy."

With those words, he buries his face between my thighs—so lush, so drenched in sweetness it seems to bloom beneath his touch. His tongue moves with precision and intent through my bottom lips, tracing every ridge and curve, learning a sacred book written in flavor and sensation, determined to leave no part of the offering untouched.

Each stroke of his tongue sends tiny tremors straight to my chest. He gripped my thighs with a possessive steadiness—anchoring me, keeping me grounded in the intensity of it all. My spine arches involuntarily, clutching the sheets—the only thing tethering me to reality—as each wave of sensation threatens to drag me deeper into the abyss.

He devours every part of me, owning every note with meticulous adoration, a secret promise in every languid motion that he will not stop until I am trembling, undone, and carved open entirely by pleasure. He feasts on me with the kind of focus that borders on violence, trying to consume the forbidden fruit itself.

My body bucks beneath him while his grip only tightens, fingers bruising into my thighs to keep me exactly where he wants me—spread, exposed, helpless to the devotion he offers with his mouth. My vision blurs, my thoughts scatter—he is unmaking me, piece by piece.

When I dare to look down, his eyes catch mine—wild, ravenous, born to break me apart and make me beg for it. And I do. Not with words, but with the desperate way my hips rise to meet his mouth again and again. His tongue moved in slow, hypnotic circles, dragging pleasure from the deepest corners of me, coaxing my body to tremble beneath the weight of his focus.

He drags his tongue over my clit one last time—before lifting his head, his mouth slick, his breathing erratic. His jaw flexes like he is barely hanging on to control. His eyes... his eyes are pure chaos. They burn into me, pinning me down harder than his hands ever could.

"I could fucking die here," he murmurs. "Bury my mouth between your thighs and call it a damn good death."

As I smile while rolling my eyes, I hear Julian's lame sobs getting out of control. It is almost funny, if it weren't so fucked up. The desperation radiates from him and I don't have to look to know he is breaking.

Xan's voice cuts through the mess.

"Oh my God, will you shut the fuck up? You had one goddamn job, Beckett," he spits. "Please her. Protect her. Fuck her like she mattered. Instead, you bored her senseless, sold her to some rich prick and tried to call it romance."

He laughs, but there is nothing warm about it. It's a sound that strikes.

"If you didn't want another man to make her moan in front of you, maybe you should have touched her like a gentleman. Not like some sad little boy hoping for gold stars and pity kisses."

Xan does not even bother to turn around. He is too busy soaking in control, enjoying every second of this. He knows what he is doing, knows just how to twist the knife.

"She's mine now. You were never good enough to start with and I'm going to fuck her the way you couldn't even dream of."

I am not sure why I cannot look away. Maybe it is the rage, the way Xan owns the room with every word, every step. This twisted satisfaction as I hear Julian fall apart, I can't help it.

"Now stay the fuck down, shut that garbage that you call your mouth, and enjoy the show, Romeo. *Oh* and, spoiler alert: my cock's going to feel way better than yours."

The moment his words leave his lips, the silence is razor-sharp. My breath catches somewhere between a gasp and a laugh, and I swear I can feel every molecule in the room vibrating. I tremble—not from fear, not even from anticipation—but from the overwhelming, wicked thrill of being wanted like this. Possessed like this.

Xan stays rooted, ignoring Julian completely, perched above me on the bed, his eyes now fixed on mine.

"You ready for him to see what it looks like when someone actually knows what the fuck they're doing?" he lets out, teeth grazing my thighs.

He notices that my legs shake, traitorous and frail. Of course he does. A cruel smirk twists on his lips as he climbs up my body, the drag of his chest against mine leaving my skin burning with need. Every part of him moves with intention. He wants me to feel every shift of muscle, every second of the turmoil he is about to unleash. His hand wraps around my throat and leans in so closely I can taste the remnants of myself on his lips.

"I warned you, Mira," he growls, his voice a dark rumble that vibes through my ribs. "You woke something dangerously feral."

"That's what I've wanted since the night you brushed past me on that street, Xan..."

His gaze darkens with a subtle smile.

"And from that second, little fox, I knew—I was going to ruin you beautifully."

The moment I have been waiting for so long arrives as he *finally* enters me—not as a conqueror, but as a man who already knows every hidden ache I carry and intends to ease them all, one push at a time. My back arches against the mattress, muscles taut and trembling while he slams into me with a force that feels almost punishing, still so perfectly right. Each thrust a wonderful brutal rhythm that leaves no room for anything but him. My fingers dig into the sheets, clawing for sanity that's already long gone, torn away the second his mouth touched my breast.

He stays silent. There is no need—everything he is saying is written in the way his body claims mine. I am a promise he has kept hidden too long, a prayer he has finally allowed himself as

235

a God to answer. His breath hits the hollow of my throat, warm and ragged, while the obscene sound of our bodies colliding fills the surrounding space.

I try to hold onto something—my name, the room, the moment—but I am unraveling completely. My moans are broken things, ripped from my chest. He watches every second, eyes locked on mine, dragging me under with nothing but a look.

"Do you realize how you were perfectly created for me?" he growls into my ear. "Knows this isn't just lust, little fox—it's fate. It's ownership. You're mine, Mira. Fucking mine. Forever."

All I can do is nod—wordless, undone—a single tear trails down my cheek, born of pain, pleasure, and something perilously close to joy. Because nothing has ever felt more devastatingly right than being shattered under the weight of his obsession. His words still echo buried inside, thudding through my chest like a second heartbeat—louder, rawer, undeniably his.

My skin hums with every syllable as his teeth grind my collarbone, then sink in just enough to make me cry out. One hand pins my wrists above my head, the other drags down between my ribs and hips.

Each thrust feels like a vow. There is no mercy, just the fever of a man crumbling with purpose. My body strains, desperate to feel him fully, to take more, to give more, until there is nothing left but us—twisted together in this beautiful, violent need.

He watches, those eyes beneath the mask locking on mine, daring me to look away, to deny what this is. Stopping now is not an option. Because this—this is what I have been drawn to my entire life.

"You feel that?" he grits out. "That's what it means to be mine."

I *do* feel it. In my lungs, in my pulse, in the trembling between my legs that's edging toward the unbearable. My cry tears from my throat—I gasp, my nails dragging down his back as my body pulses around him. He knows exactly what he is doing—how to bring me so close I am trembling, begging, unable to think of anything, but how much more I need.

"This feels so good Xan," I manage to whisper, cracked and soaked in need. "Don't you *dare* stop."

The sound of our bodies colliding fills the room. My fingers trace the sharp edges of his mask, desperate to see more, to feel more. He pauses, his breath catching. Clearly, my touch has struck something under his skin.

"Please," I whisper, trembling with an untamable need. "Let me have this. Just once."

His jaw tightens. I see it—the war behind Xan's eyes. That pull between instinct and duty, desire and control. His longing is written all over him. Still, he hesitates. Because to lift the mask is to expose more than his face—it's exposing the man beneath the monster. I slide closer, until my body melts against his, until my breath mingles with the perfume on his neck. I tilt my face up, eyes never leaving his.

"You don't understand, Xan..." I soften, smoky with emotion. "I *need* this. I *need* to feel your mouth against mine like I need air. After everything—after what you have done to me, *for* me—I want to know the taste of the man who destroyed and rebuilt me all at once."

He swallows hard, his hands twitching at his sides, torn.

"I've kissed lies my whole life," I continue, bolder now, letting my fingertips graze the bottom of his mask, "but I know yours would be the only truth. And I want to drown in it."

Still nothing.

I let my lips ghost along his jaw, just below the leather.

"Let me worship you, Xan. Let me know you, not the mask. Just for this moment, I beg you."

A beat.

Another.

Then, with an intense growl, he lifts it—just high enough to set his mouth free. And God, when his lips finally crush into mine, it is not just a kiss—it's a storm. One I begged for. One I welcome.

His mouth crashes into mine with a force that steals every thought from my mind. No gentleness softens his kiss—only urgency and hunger held back for far too long. His lips are scorching, sculpting mine with a centuries-deep hunger for this contact.

His hand grips the side of my neck, tilting my head just enough to deepen the kiss, his thumb pressing into the hollow beneath my jaw. I melt under his touch, every nerve set ablaze as his tongue claims the corners of my mouth with punishing precision. He kisses as if it is the only language he has ever known, and I understand every word.

I cling to his shoulders, fingers digging into the tense curve of his muscles while our breaths tangle, hot and reckless. I swear I can taste every unspoken thing he has never dared to say. Every truth buried beneath leather and silence.

He doesn't pull away out of doubt—only to breathe. But even then, his forehead rests against mine, his lips hovering just above mine.

"I swore myself I would never do this," he murmurs, "but *you,* little fox... you make it fucking impossible."

"I don't want you to resist me," I say back, my hands sliding to cup his face beneath the mask. "Not when this feels like everything I've ever needed."

He kisses me again. Slower this time—more devout. He's savoring the sacredness of the moment, because he knows this kiss is a line neither of us will ever come back from.

"You're close, aren't you?" he asks. "I can feel it... your pussy throbbing around my dick for more."

Again, all I can do is nod, my voice lost in the tightness of my chest, in the delicious ache building inside me. My hands fist in his hair—anything I can hold onto as I feel myself slipping away. He angles his hips just right, and the friction becomes too much.

"I'm about to come baby," I cried out softly. "And I want you to come with me, inside me. I want to feel every drop of your cum flooding my thighs."

Xan lets out a soundless chuckle between his ragged breaths. "I wouldn't have wanted it any other way little fox," he hisses.

A shock of pleasure surges, and I cry out loud as the orgasm tears through me with an intensity I never experienced before. My body bows into his, clenching, falling apart completely in his grasp. He follows with a guttural moan, deep and animalistic, burying himself to the hilt as he releases his precious cum into me, holding me so tightly it feels like we might fuse together. As we were never meant to be anything but this. My chest rises and falls in erratic waves. His body is still wrapped around mine, though it is the chaos he has left inside me that holds me prisoner.

I am supposed to feel used, to feel ashamed, even afraid. Still, all I feel is... alive. Split open and stitched back together by the hands of a man who knows exactly where every fracture lies. Julian never touched this part of me—not really. He danced around it, tried to mold it, shame it, silence it.

But Xan? Xan did not ask for permission to enter the dark. He kicked the door off its hinges and made a home in it.

And God *help* me... I want him to stay.

Xan groans, still catching his air, then glances down at me with a smirk that could cut glass.

"Look at you, little fox. Fucked-out and glowing—I guess I just gave you a whole new definition of pleasure, *huh?*"

He leans down, pressing a slow, claiming kiss just beneath my jaw.

"And to think, all that time you wasted with Julian and his participation trophy dick."

His fingers drift lazily over my hip, possessive even in their tenderness.

"Don't worry, Mira... I'll make sure you never forget what love is supposed to feel like."

Chapter 24

XAN

*T*he aftermath is something to relish. There is nothing quite like lying next to your partner, lighting a cigarette, and letting the world fall away as we both sink into the post-coital silence.

The smoke curls up, filling the space, and for a moment, it's just us—no words—just pure satisfaction. But tonight, the usual peace I crave after is nowhere to be found, thanks to that bitch, who is slowly bleeding out at the foot of the bed.

I turn to Mira as she sits up to run my fingers gently down her bare back. The calm that should be ours feels tainted; the stillness of the room filled with the faint sound of Julian's struggle.

Goosebumps rise on Mira's skin, and I cannot help but imagine how her breast must look from his vantage point, the thought of it filling me with a burning rage that I can barely keep contained. I grab my hoodie and drape it over her shoulders. She remains still, her eyes glued to her ex-lover, mind clearly elsewhere. I can see it in the way her brow furrows, how she is caught in a tornado of doubt. I cannot blame her—it is a lot to take in. But there is no going back now. Not when we are this far gone.

"You know he's getting exactly what he deserves, don't you?" I ask Mira calmly, yet authoritatively. "My approach may be harsh, though it is far from unjustified."

I see her gaze drop to the floor.

"You're not doing anything to him he did not bring upon himself. He's a fucking loser. You deserve nothing less than the best, little fox."

Her body shivers increasingly and after a moment of reluctance, she gets up. I stay quiet, letting her take the lead, my eyes tracing every movement she makes. Julian's gaze widens, a mix of fear and anticipation hanging, wondering what is coming next.

She stands beside him; her figure looming over like a silent executioner. The knife gleams in her hand, a dangerous reflection of her determination.

Swiftly, she pulls off the tape, the sound of it tearing through the room. There is a subtle tremor in her fingers as she places the blade just close enough to remind him of the power she now holds. Julian's eyes widen with distress. Sadly for him, there is no mercy in hers—just cold, controlled resolve.

"*Please*, Mira, stop! I'm... I'm sorry! I swear, I didn't mean it! Don't... don't do this—it's not who you are!"

His words come out in a frantic rush, each one dripping with the desperation of a man who is aware he is spiraling down. His eyes are darting between her and the blade, a flicker of agony as he tries to cling to any shred of hope. Mira's laughter erupts, jagged and manic, as her voice quivers with fury.

"*Not who I am?* You don't know a fucking thing about me!" she spits, her words like daggers aimed at him. "You never gave a damn to figure out who I really was. Maybe if I had a goddamn dollar sign branded on my forehead, you would have bothered to listen!"

Her chest heaves with rage, and her grip on the knife tightens, as if it is the only thing keeping her tethered to some semblance of control. Her eyes blaze with a fire born of years of resentment as she takes a step closer. Despite everything, I cannot help but get hard again, the intensity of Mira's wrath almost makes me forget the gravity of what we are doing.

Seeing her like this, taking the reign of her own destiny, her skin glistening with sweat, her wild red hair tumbling in disarray, naked and unrestrained—not once I have seen anything so beautiful. She radiates a newfound strength, reborn right here and now, and I am truly captivated—pulled toward her in ways I never expected.

With every word she spits, my body stiffens, the tension coursing through my legs and I am compelled beyond reason, I seize the primal surge that consumes me. I massage my cock with intense fervor, veins straining under the pressure, pulsing like a wild heartbeat.

"You always shoved me aside, like I was some fucking afterthought. You always had something more important. Well, guess what? I'm done being your second choice."

I watch her, spellbound, as she hovers over him—Julian, strapped down, powerless, reduced to nothing more than a whimpering heap at her feet.

There is no escape for him. No mercy coming.

Only her.

Fuck, I have seen nothing more feral, more perfect.

Julian thrashes weakly against the restraints, his wrists already bleeding. His voice cracks from crying.

"I was scared, Mira!" he croaks out, desperate. "I didn't mean to—I didn't know how to—"

"You didn't know how to treat a human being, you mean," she cuts him off coldly. "You didn't know how to love something unless it stayed quiet and easy to manage."

He shakes his head violently, choking on his own panic.

"I loved you! I did—I swear—"

"You loved the *idea* of me," she spits. "You loved what you could use. You loved how easy it was to make me feel like nothing."

She crouches down and I can see the moment Julian realizes she is not just talking anymore—she's choosing.

"You made me feel like shit," she repeats, quieter now. "But I am not nothing. I am everything you were too small to even fucking dream about."

Julian sobs harder, pulling helplessly at the ropes binding him to the frame.

"Please, Mira, *please*—this isn't you, you're not like this—"

Her smile is pure fucking nightmare fuel.

"No," she whispers. "I'm better."

Behind her, I grip my cock, painfully hard, watching her claim every shred of her destiny back—damn, she is magnificently violent. Julian squirms weakly against the restraints, a pitiful sound tearing from his throat as Mira stands over him, the knife glinting wickedly in her hand.

Julian's face crumples, blood smearing the corners of his mouth.

"Mira, FUCK, please—"

He whimpers, sagging lower. She steps even closer, until the tip of the knife kisses his throat, trembling from the force of her fury.

"I gave you everything, my mind, my soul, my skin," she says, venom dripping from every word. "And you repaid me with empty promises and cold beds. So, tell me Julian..."

She leans in, her mouth right by his ear, her hair brushing his bloody cheek. "Who's disposable now?"

Julian suddenly lets out a laugh—high-pitched, broken, almost maniacal.

"You think you're so invincible now?" he chokes out, his lips cracked and bleeding. "Look at you... miserable. All that anger—for what? You were never enough. Not then. Not now, nor ever!"

He spits blood to the side, sneering up at her with hollow eyes.

"You think you broke me, sweetie? You couldn't even *satisfy* me. You are nothing, Mira! Just a fucking tight hole I couldn't even use and a pretty face."

I see Mira's shoulders contract, the blade trembling slightly in her hand—rage and heartbreak colliding in real time.

She's slipping.

Enough.

I step up beside her; the floor creaking under my weight, my hand ghosting the small of her back.

You're not alone, little fox.

Julian's sneer falters the second he feels my presence. I lean close to her ear.

"Make him fucking gargle his last breath."

Her knuckles whiten around the handle while towering over what is left of him—a pitiful, broken thing, no more threat than a stray hissing at a lioness.

Julian tries to twist away,

"DAMN Mira, wait—PLEASE—!"

But she is already moving.

No mercy.

No more hesitation.

Game over.

The blade slides deep across his neck with a sickening ease. A wet, gurgling sound claws at the air before everything goes eerily still. He winces as the blood seeps, his last gasp fills the room and eyes widen. Mira just stands there, trembling, bathed in the aftermath, the knife slipping from her fingers and clattering to the floor. I catch her before she can collapse, wrapping her against me so fiercely, her skin fever-hot against mine.

My heart is a fucking war drum in my chest, hammering so loud I can taste copper on my tongue. A raw, instinctive part of me is filled with pride.

Look at her. Look at what she just did.

My little fox.

I nuzzle into the curve where her shoulder meets her neck, inhaling her sweat, her fear, her triumph. I don't give a fuck that Julian's corpse is still bleeding out at our feet.

Let it bleed. Let the whole fucking world burn.

I tilt her chin up roughly, forcing her to meet my eyes. She is dazed, tears clinging to her lashes, but she has never looked freer.

More mine.

"You did it," I let out. "You chose yourself. You chose *us,* baby."

She blinks, shivering, still lost somewhere between shock and euphoria. I lean down, brushing my forehead on hers with a tenderness that feels almost savage after everything we have just unleashed. She just buries her face against my chest, small gasps tearing from her lips, and it guts me.

"You're okay, little fox," I whisper against her hair. "You're safe. I've got you."

I scoop her into my arms, cradling her onto my torso like the precious treasure she is. Then, I walk toward the corridor to kick open the bathroom door to set her down inside. She sways on her feet while I keep a hand wrapped around her waist to steady her. The hot water roars to life, steam filling the small space.

I grab a cloth and start cleaning her carefully, washing away every drop of blood. Her skin pebbles under my touch. Goosebumps everywhere.

Never once does she pull away. I catch a glimpse of her reflection in the foggy mirror—wide, hollow eyes.

She is *mine.*

Mine to protect.

She is also mine to put back together.

When I'm done, I wrap her tight in a towel, lift her again, and carry her out like she weighs nothing. I settle Mira onto the couch, tucking the bath sheet around my girl. She curls up instantly, fists clenching the fabric as if it is the only thing tethering her to the world. I kneel in front of her, brushing a damp strand of hair from her face.

"I'm right here," I tell her, voice low. "I'm not going anywhere, ever."

I stay there for a long moment, just watching her breathe until I finally pull away and grab my phone.

> Need premium cleaning ASAP, sending the coordinate.

I wipe my hands off and lean back against the kitchen counter, watching her sleep on the couch. Still nestled in place, still haunted.

> It's done.

A pause. Lucian's never fast, but he always answers.

How did she look after?

> Like hell. Like she crossed a line and knew she couldn't go back. But she held steady.

I glance over at her. Her hair's stuck to her cheek. There's a streak of blood near her collarbone I did not manage to clean off.

So, you really believe the foxling is ready?

I grit my teeth.

> I'm not asking for permission. She earned her place. The hard way.

Lol, that's rich, coming from you. The golden son, hand-fed by the Order.

> And yet I did my time. More than anyone. She's tougher than half the cowards in your ranks—and she didn't need a damn mask to do it.

> You're too attached.

I glare at the screen like it just called me a simp.

Attached? *Please.* I have practically engraved her name on my ribcage—but I am not going to give Lucian the satisfaction of knowing that.

> I'm loyal, big difference.

> Careful, Xan. Loyalty is one thing.
> Attachment is rot.

I almost laugh. That says it all, doesn't it? A man who spits out a line like that could never love anyone—only owning, controlling, corrupting.

> Then pray she never turns on you. Because if she does, you won't see it coming.

Another silence. A longer one.

> Bring her in. Let's see what your little fox will do when the wolves come for her.

I sit down beside her, careful not to wake her as I lower myself onto the verge of the couch. She is curled in on herself, her hair's still damp, skin flushed from the heat of the shower—and everything that came before it.

253

For a long time, I just stare. Watching the slow rise and fall of her chest. The faint crease between her brows, even in sleep, her body's still holding on to some last shred of fear or rage. I want to smooth it away with my thumb. I want to carve the world clean, so she never has to wear that expression again.

This girl walked into my life like a goddamn match dropped in gasoline. And instead of running from the flames, I lit one right back. I have killed for her. Lied for her. I just watched her become darker and stronger than anyone thought she could be— and fuck, I have wanted nothing more than I want *this*. Her. A future. Something real in the wreckage.

I was not supposed to feel this way. Was not supposed to let her in. But I see it now. Clear as day. She is not just a mission anymore.

She is the whole fucking reason.

Chapter 25

MIRA

I wake up with a heavy head, the kind of dull fog that clings to you after too much sleep—or maybe too much alcohol. The sunlight bleeding through the curtains tells me it is morning. Not just early morning. Late. I have slept straight through the night like a corpse, unmoving and unaware.

Yesterday.

Oh, God—*yesterday.*

The realization slams into my head, and I jolt upright so fast the room tilts. My heart is already racing as I stumble to my feet, legs shaky with panic and confusion.

I rush to my bedroom. It might still hold evidence of what I did—what I became. But the moment I burst through the door, my breath catches.

Everything is... spotless.

No blood. No broken glass. No ropes or knife. Not a single drop of Julian's existence remains. The carpet is clean. The bed is made. The air smells faintly of citrus, not even a trace of Xan. No sign of the madness we unleashed. No sign of the first time I let him take me, mind and body.

It is like nothing ever happened.

I stand there in stunned silence, trying to process the disconnect. My mind races to fill in the blanks, to explain away the gaping hole between memory and reality. Maybe I drank too much. Maybe this was some twisted hallucination—some elaborate nightmare conjured by guilt, wine and trauma. The human brain is terrifying like that. It can make you believe anything. And part of me wants to buy it. Because the alternative?

That I killed Julian.

That I watched him bleed.

That I let Xan drag me to hell and liked the taste of the abyss?

That is harder to face.

My body is still humming from the aftershocks of it all, yet my mind is scrambling to tell me it was just a dream.

Awesome. I either invented the world's most deranged wet dream... or I committed murder and got laid by my stalker on the same night.

So, why does my body ache like it happened? Why does my throat feel like I screamed? And why the hell do I still smell his cologne? The perfume of all sins dressed in silk with smoke, dark spices and leather.

I look at my reflection on the way out.

Hair: *chaos*. Skin: *flushed*. Eyes: *haunted*.

If this is my subconscious at work, she is a troubled bitch with a flair for cinematic detail. I should feel relief. I should laugh it off, call Zoey, book a spa day, do anything remotely normal. Instead, I find myself looking for something more. Anything. A clue. A wrinkle in the fabric of reality. Because what scares me most is not that it was real.

It's that I want it to be.

I pull my hair into a messy knot, trying to shake off the weight in my skull. But when I catch my reflection in the mirror, I freeze.

There—just at the beginning of my neck. Faint. Faded. Yet unmistakable. A handprint. My fingers brush over it, and suddenly a flash hits me—hot breath against my skin. A grip tightening just as his mouth found mine. My legs wrapped around him, the sound of skin, of teeth, of his voice—low, praising, filthy.

I blink, and it is gone. It had to be a dream. Right?

Right?

I stare at myself again, unblinking this time. The handprint remains. Soft bruising, just enough to show fingertips splayed along my throat, curving beneath my jaw like a collar. Not accidental. Not imagined.

Intentional.

My pulse flutters beneath it like a trapped bird. I can almost feel his possessive hand again. I drag my fingers over the marks, and now I know for certain—this was not a dream. I did not imagine it. I did not imagine the way he looked at me, I the way he touched me. And I definitely did not imagine the way I wanted it.

Still want it.

Shame creeps in. I swallow it down. There is no blood. No Julian. No mess. The apartment is faultless. *Sterile.* Like nothing ever happened. Like someone came through and erased the anarchy with surgical precision.

Though they did not erase me. Not the bruises. Not the ache in my body. Nor the image of Xan, mouth against my throat, whispering things no one should want to hear—and yet I did.

Oh God, I did.

I am still standing there, half-dressed, fingers ghosting over my neck. When I hear the soft click of the door, I spin.

There he is. Leaning against the frame like he owns the air in the room. Black shirt. Dark eyes. That same maddening calm stretched over something entirely unhinged. His gaze drops to my throat—just for a second, he sees my neck. He knows. He smiles. I can tell by the look in his eyes. A knowing, dangerous smile that makes the mark on my skin burn hotter.

"Morning, little fox," he says roughly from sleep or smoke or maybe both. He steps closer, slowly, as if I'll bolt.

"What... what happened last night," I breathe. "Was it real?"

He stops inches away, looking down at me.

"You tell me," he murmurs, lifting a hand, just to hover right over the fading imprint he left behind.

"I did not dream that," I whisper.

"No," he says. "You did not."

My knees almost buckle. "I—Julian—"

"Gone," he cuts in, gently but firmly. "You don't need to think about that coward hurting you anymore."

Gone? *How* gone?

I stare at him. At the man who turned my world inside out and made me want it that way. Xan's gaze switches heavier, an ominous shadow passing over his features as he locks eyes with me. His expression says it all—he knows exactly what lurks behind my silence. He knows what I'm feeling, even when I cannot bring myself to voice it. The anxiety. The doubt...

"You want to know what happened to your ex, *huh?*" he leans in slightly, as though waiting for permission to continue.

I clench my fists. It is hard to admit, but I need to know.

"Yes," I whisper, my throat tight. "I really need to know."

"The Order doesn't do things delicately, Mira," he says with a touch of sarcasm. "Especially when it comes to a scum like Beckett."

His fingers briefly graze the mark on my neck as he leans back, his eyes dark with something unreadable as he studies me.

"Julian's body... Let's say it's dealt with," Xan continues in a low measured tone. "He won't be found. The Order and I made sure of it."

I am not certain whether I should feel relieved or horrified. The idea of his body disappearing, of everything vanishing without a trace, makes my stomach twist. It should be comforting—knowing that whatever happened, whatever he deserved, is gone. Still a part of me, the part I cannot quite silence, feels... wrong. There is no closure. No finality. Xan watches my reaction closely.

"You're quiet," he remarks. "Did you really think we would just leave the mess?"

I hesitate, my mind racing, trying to process everything. His words are like a cold splash of water, and yet... there is something strangely reassuring in the way he speaks about it. As though violence was just another part of their world, one I'd been unwilling to face until now.

"I didn't expect... I... I don't know what I expected actually," I say, my voice cracking slightly. "I just... I thought it would be harder. I thought... there would be more to it. I don't know."

He steps closer, the heat of his body warming the space between us. Gently, his hand comes up to touch my face, his thumb brushing against my cheek tenderly.

"Well, if you need to know more, Mira, let me help you," he retorts. "Are you aware of what hydrochloric acid does? Do you know it can make absolutely *anything* disappear? It doesn't explode. It just—melts everything. Metal, wood, *flesh*—it doesn't care. It seeps in, burns through, turning skin to pulp, bone to mush. One second, something's whole, and the next, it's reduced to nothing but a puddle, a mass of liquefied remains. No scream. No blood. Just the slow, agonizing disappearance into nothingness."

My gut clenches with dread.

"I'm not saying that's what happened. I'm just stating a fact. Purely educational, really."

A ghost of a smirk tugs in his eyes. He knows how fucked up it sounds—and he is enjoying every second of my reaction.

"Listen, you have been in this world only for a short moment," Xan murmurs gentle now, the sarcasm gone. "But enough for you to have seen things. Done things. This... this is just another part of it. Another step you have to take."

No response comes to mind. Part of me wants to escape this new life, to flee the blood, the violence that is supposed to become so normal. However, another part—the part that is connected to him, the part that is terrified of facing the truth—knows that I can't. Not anymore.

"I never wanted this," I whisper, barely audible.

Xan does not respond at first. Instead, he takes a step back, running a hand through his hair in that familiar gesture of impatience. When his eyes find mine again, they carry something different. Something gentler—close to understanding.

"No one ever does," he says quietly. "But you're here. And this... it's your reality from now on."

I close my eyes, the weight of his words pressing down on me. What's done is done. Julian will not come back, and neither will who I was before. I am still breathing, that is what matters.

I don't know how long I stood there, feeling the gravity of everything we've made, everything I have become. When I open my eyes again, Xan is still watching me.

"You want to know what happens next?" he asks, cutting through the silence.

I nod slowly, not trusting myself to speak.

"Well now," he says with a glint in his eye, "we continue your ascension, little fox."

Chapter 26

MIRA

I was not sure what I was expecting—but it definitely was not this.

The building is nothing like I imagined. From the outside, it's a fortress. Cold, imposing. The walls are not the familiar red brick I have seen in Brooklyn's older buildings; they are charcoal-gray, almost black. The kind of color that swallows the light, leaving the whole place drenched in shadow. The windows, narrow and grimy, are covered in what looks like years of neglect. It is as if the building's been standing here forever, untouched by time.

The street is quiet, too quiet. No hustle, no noise of life. Just the low hum of the city a few blocks away. Even that feels distant, muted. This place feels forgotten by the world. I guess that is the point.

Xan is walking beside me, his presence solid and unwavering, yet I can feel the tension in his step. His eyes are scanning the surroundings, alert, as if expecting anything or anyone to jump out of the dark. He leads me through an old iron door; the metal screeching slightly as it opens.

The moment we step inside, I feel the shift. Immediately, the room sucks the air out of my lungs. The space is cavernous, endless, yet suffocating, with its high dark ceilings and the shadowy corners that stretch on forever. The floor is cold beneath my feet, the wood worn and untouched by a mop in what looks like years. The lights flicker overhead, their dim glow casting everything in an eerie, almost haunting hue.

It is not the atmosphere that makes my heart pound the most—it's the people. Every man who looks at me—*because every single one of them does*—is wearing the same mask.

Sleek. Black. Leather.

No mouth, no expression, just two dark eye slits and smooth, seamless lines stretched over bone and intent. A mask that does not hide identity—it erases humanity. They all wear it. Like a uniform. Like a warning. Identical and faceless, yet somehow each gaze feels more ravenous than the last.

Predators in tailored black.

And I? I am the only one unmasked. *Exposed.*

I hear the hushed murmurs the instant we enter. A wave of heat rises to my face as I feel dozens of pairs of eyes latch onto us, like creatures scenting blood. There is not even a pretense of hiding it. I can practically hear them salivating.

They're circling.

The room is a sea of motionless bodies, yet every one of them is taut with tension, ready to strike. There is a hunger in their gaze, a kind of primitive thirst impossible to ignore.

I have just stepped into the wolf's den.

I can feel their eyes on me, stripping me down, analyzing, dissecting. They are not just curious—they are calculating. They want to know why I am here. They want to see if I am worthy. And the sickest part? They're not even hiding it.

They want to possess me.

I glance up at Xan. His body is like a wall next to mine, tense, vibrating with restraint. His hand slides down my back, not gently, but with a pressure that says I am his. A growl rumbles in his chest, barely audible. His head sweeps over the room, locking onto the closest group of watchers as I feel a tension thick enough to cut. His presence is magnetic, the type of force that commands space without a single word.

"They're fucking starving," he says, barely loud enough for me to hear. His grip tightens, a silent warning. "Like wolves on a fresh kill. And they will tear into you if you show any sign of weakness. Don't give them the satisfaction."

I swallow hard, my pulse quickening. I have stepped into a hive of predators, and they all want a piece of me, clearly *not* in a *Britney Spears* kind of way. This is not attraction—it is a power play, a test of dominance, and I have just stepped in as the next prey.

Xan pulls me closer, his body practically enveloping mine as he guides me forward, moving with purpose, not an ounce of hesitation in his stride. The crowd parts as we walk through, their gazes following us like a ripple through the water, unblinking, unyielding.

One man—tall, with icy eyes and a smirk in them that screams arrogance—takes a step forward. He wants to speak, but Xan is faster.

"Keep your fucking distance if you want to keep your head attached to your damn body."

The room goes quiet. Every stare is on us now, but I refuse to look away. I cannot. Because if I do, if I show any crack in my armor, if I show the slightest sign of fear, I know exactly what will happen.

As we continue our path through the hall, I realize—he is not just protecting me. He is asserting domination, reminding them all who is in control here.

Earlier this morning, I finally gave in to Xan's invitation to the Order. Part of me was deeply curious—curious to see the man who orchestrated everything from the shadows. The man behind the strings, the silence, the chaos. More than anything, I want to ask him *why*. Not that I expect a straight answer—men like him do not speak in truths. But maybe, just maybe, I could catch something in his words. A glimpse. A thread I could pull to make sense of it all.

According to Xan, I already have everything it takes to be accepted. He says it with such conviction as if it was already written in stone. He believes in me in a way that feels... foreign. Fierce. Loud. Much louder than the whispering doubts that have lived in me for years...

It is hard to explain what it does to a person—to be raised by a parent who clipped your wings before you even knew how to fly. To love a person who made you question every part of yourself. It carves wounds you forget are there, leaves you second-guessing even your own reflection. You call it survival. But in truth, it's just slow erosion.

Yet—Xan sees past that, somehow. Bit by bit, he chips away at the rot they left behind and replaces it with something else. Strength. Unapologetic, sharpened strength. He is not just helping me stand. He is showing me how to rebuild. For that... I am endlessly, quietly grateful. Even if I do not know how to say it yet.

We walk past the now complete silence of the common hall, where masks follow me like shadows. Xan doesn't say a word as he leads me down a narrow hallway, each step echoing over stone tiles. My pulse taps at my throat. It should not feel this ceremonial, and yet... it does. Like I am about to be judged, weighed, and possibly discarded.

We stop at a tall black door, aged but polished, its wood marked by time and secrets. Xan knocks once—not out of courtesy, but as a signal.

"Enter," comes the unbothered calm voice from inside.

Xan pushes open the door and guides me in with a firm hand on my back. I barely cross the threshold before I find myself in front of *him*.

Lucian Voss.

He is standing by a floor-to-ceiling window, back turned, hands clasped behind him like he is orchestrating the entire goddamn world from that single spot. The room is lit only by the pale light of morning filtering through the window and the soft flicker of one antique lamp.

He turns slowly, his gaze landing on me. His mask is like the others, but silver, smooth and gleaming like a blade in the dark. It catches the light just enough to look alive. Behind it, his gaze burns with a steady, merciless fire. His hair is long blond silvered, slicked back, and his suit is perfectly tailored—a dark grey three-piece that fits him like skin. His presence is utterly magnetic.

"The infamous Mira Vale," he says smoothly.

His face remains hidden, unreadable—but I swear I can feel the daring in his tone. I nod once, doing my best not to shrink under his scrutiny.

"I've heard quite a bit about you."

I lift my chin with the last fragile scrap of courage I can muster.

"Then you must know I have questions." Lucian walks forward.

"Of course you do. Anyone worth recruiting usually does."

Recruiting.

The word hits me in the gut. Xan shifts protectively beside me, but silent. Lucian stops a few feet in front of me.

"Before I answer anything... I want to see if you are brave enough to ask the right questions."

Brave enough? The nerve, after all they had me endure.

"Alright then. Here's one—how long have I been watched? Before Julian. Before Xan."

Lucian's eyes glint, like I have said something amusing. Or perhaps dangerous.

"A long time," he says simply. "Longer than you'd like to believe."

A chill snakes down my spine.

"And why me?" I ask, stepping forward before I lose my nerve. "Why keep tabs on a woman who's never done anything extraordinary?"

Lucian's smile sharpens, his intrigued eyes narrowing slightly.

"You still believe that?", he says, almost to himself. "You think you are ordinary? That's adorable."

Xan tenses beside me. I can feel he is holding back. Letting me speak. Letting me stand for myself. Lucian continues.

"You were born into something bigger than yourself, Mira. You have spent your whole life running from shadows you didn't even know had names. But we knew. I knew. And now, whether you like it or not, you're standing at our mercy."

He leans in. "The question isn't why *you*. It's... why not sooner?"

I open my mouth, but nothing comes out. Because deep down, some part of me—some fractured, hidden part—already knew I did not walk into this by accident. I was brought here for a reason.

Lucian straightens, brushing invisible dust off his sleeve.

"Ask your next question carefully, Mira Vale. Each one peels back a layer. And not all truths are kind."

I wet my lips, pulse still hammering behind my ribs.

"I don't want riddles," I say. "I want clarity. What exactly does the Order expect from me?"

Lucian delays his response. He studies me instead, like he is measuring something—my resolve, maybe. Or my ignorance.

"We expect loyalty," he finally says, walking away. "Discipline. Obedience, in time."

I hold back a scoff.

"*Obedience*? I'm not a fucking soldier."

He turns his head slightly, just enough for me to catch the flicker of amusement on his face.

"No. You're something far more dangerous."

I freeze at that, a tight breath catching in my lungs.

Lucian gestures toward me, fingers like a puppeteer.

"You have the potential to be useful in ways most here never will. Not because of what you are now... but because of what you could become. We cultivate that."

My skin crawls.

"Useful how?"

Xan shifts beside me. His arm brushes mine, just enough to ground me. He wants me to stand in this. To face it.

Lucian speaks again, softer this time.

"You came here asking for truth. But the truth has teeth, Mira. And it will not bite gently."

That last sentence lands hard. I draw a slow breath.

"So, I'm a project. A tool to be molded."

His smile returns, elegant and bloodless.

"No, Mira. You're not a tool." He leans forward. "You're an investment."

My heart is thudding, trying to beat the truth out of me, but I keep my face still. I have no idea what kind of game Lucian is playing—or how many pieces are already on the board, but I know this: I'm not the one holding the rules. I turn to Xan. He looks calm, but I know it is an act.

"I'm not afraid of purpose," I finally say, carefully. "Doesn't mean I enjoy walking blind."

Lucian laughs just barely.

"You'll have sight soon enough."

Something about the way he says it makes my stomach knot. Still, I just nod, holding back the scream clawing its way up. If they are waiting for me to prove something, *fine*.

Let them wait.

Let them wonder.

I will find out what this is really about. And when I do, I won't be the girl fumbling in the dark. I will be the one lighting the match.

Lucian turns away, his focus shifting to the window, as if I no longer matter.

"You'll stay here. We have rooms. Someone will show you."

Stay?

I blink. "Just like that?"

He glances over his shoulder.

"What were you expecting. Chains? A blindfold? I am not like your boyfriend."

"No," I say, sharper than I intended. "But maybe a reason why."

Lucian smiles without humor.

"You'll get your reason soon enough. For now, consider this your... initiation period."

Of course, that sounds totally reassuring. Before I can press further, he waves a hand toward the door. Xan's already stepped forward, sensing the moment. His fingers brush the small of my back again, gentle but firm. I let him lead me out, while I keep my eyes on Lucian until the door shuts behind us.

Whatever game they are playing, I'm in it now.

And I have no intend to lose.

We don't make it ten steps before a figure rounds the corner ahead. Tall. Light brown hair. Broad-shouldered. Clad in black from neck to boots and wearing the same mask as the others—just the aura of someone who definitely owns too many knives and not enough self-awareness.

He tilts his head at me. And I mean tilts—like *head-turns-in-a-horror-movie* tilts.

"Well, well," he murmurs. "She's prettier than I expected."

In one swift, furious motion, Xan slams him against the stone wall with a forearm across his chest. The impact echoes down the corridor.

"Try that again, Kayde," Xan growls, his face inches from the man in front of him. "Say one more word about her. Look at her like that again."

Kayde.

Yeah, that is definitely a new name. And judging by the tension radiating off Xan, it is not on his Christmas card list.

Kayde lets out a breathless chuckle, as if this is foreplay.

"Easy, brother. I was just admiring the Order's newest stray. No harm in noticing a beautiful thing."

"You don't get to notice her," Xan snaps, his voice darker than I have ever heard it. "She's not yours to *notice*."

Kayde's smile shifts under the mask by the look in his eyes.

"You sure about that? Thought we didn't keep pets here."

I look between them, heart thudding, trying to catch up. "Okay. Someone want to tell me what brand of psychotic pissing contest this is?"

It is not until Xan blocks me with a swift motion that I realize I have moved.

"She's under my protection," he says, low and final.

Kayde lifts both palms like he's surrendering, but his eyes stay on me.

"That won't save her, Hayes. You know how this place works."

Xan's grip tightens—just for a second—before he shoves Kayde back against the wall and steps away.

Kayde adjusts his collar like nothing happened.

"I like her," he adds, directing it to me this time. "Hope you won't break too easily."

Then he's gone. Just like that. The silence he leaves behind buzzes. I look up at Xan, my heart hammering.

"Who was that?"

Xan exhales hard through his nose.

"Kayde Morrow. Don't you dare talk to him or listen to him. If he ever touches you, I will put him alive in the fucking ground."

I cannot help but let out a soft laugh—because his jealousy, as absurd as it is, borders on theatrical. But God, I wouldn't trade it for anything. There is something deeply satisfying about watching a man like Xan Hayes—deadly, brooding, always in control—lose his cool over me.

Totally normal. Just a man who would burn the world down if someone else looked at me for too long.

His fingers lace through mine firmly. My hand looks so small in his, delicate and breakable. By all logic, I should be scared. Yet I feel nothing.

It feels like being swallowed whole in the best possible way. *Safe.* Held together by someone who sees every jagged edge and grips tighter anyway. With his hand in mine, the planet could fall to ruin, and I would still believe in something. I would still believe in *us.*

The hallway narrows before flaring open again, revealing a series of identical doors along one side—sleek, dark, and quietly foreboding. Xan stops in front of one of them and reaches into his pocket, retrieving a small key I saw him took from a board full of them on the wall in Lucian's office. He hands it over without looking at me.

"This one's yours," he simply says.

I blink at the key in my palm.

"My room?" I ask, half-expecting him to say I misunderstood.

"It is the rule," he mutters, already sounding irritated by it. "Everyone gets their own space."

I study the door, then glance back at him.

"You don't sound thrilled at all." He shrugs, but it is sharp, tense.

"I'm not in the habit of following rules I didn't write."

The key turns with a soft click as I push the door open. The room inside is surprisingly spacious, austere, but beautiful—stone walls softened by heavy black curtains, a tall bed with clean, dark linens, and a desk pushed beneath a slender window. A flickering wall sconce casts a warm golden hue over it all. It is nothing like home.

It is better. *And worse.* Which makes it perfect.

I step inside slowly, taking in the faint scent of sandalwood and cold air. Xan stands in the doorway like a shadow that refuses to leave.

"I thought you would want somewhere to rest," he says quietly.

I turn to him. "I did. I do." But when he still does not move, I arch a brow. "Are you going to stay there all night? Or are you planning to break the rules on day one?"

He does not smile. Not really. But his eyes gleam.

"I've already broken worse ones for you."

He steps inside without waiting for an invitation, pushing the door shut behind. The room swells with his presence immediately—too large, too solid, too him.

I lean against the desk, watching him like he is some wild thing that wandered into my territory. Except we both know it is the other way around.

Xan walks closer.

"If the Order wanted me away from you, they'd have to try fucking harder than a locked door."

"I thought you said everyone gets their own space," I tease.

"I lied." He stops in front of me, close enough that the heat of him makes my breath catch. "Or maybe I just decided you'd sleep better with someone watching you."

I tilt my head, amused. "*Watching* me, or *sleeping* with me?"

"I haven't decided yet."

I should tell him to leave. That I need time to process. To think. But my fingers are already curling into his shirt, pulling him forward. He meets me halfway, one hand bracing on the desk beside me, the other sliding around my waist. When he leans in, our foreheads touch—barely.

"I know this place looks like stone and shadows," he says, his breath brushing my lips. "But you're not alone in it. Not while I'm here."

His breath lingers on my skin, teasing, testing—waiting for permission he does not really need. The world has narrowed to this one second, stretched taut between restraint and surrender.

"You're trembling, little fox," he whispers, brushing his thumb just beneath my ribs. "Is it fear... or envy?"

"Do you want a real answer?" I murmur.

He laughs—barely. "Only if it's honest."

I don't look away. "Then it's both."

That's all it takes.

Just like the night before, he lifts his mask—only enough to free his mouth. God, the way my heart stumbles—his move, his choice. He wants this. He could have held back, but he did not. His mouth crashes into mine as if he has been waiting since the moment I stepped through the Order's doors to finally kiss me.

His hands are everywhere—my waist, my back, my throat. Xan lifts me onto the desk, scattering papers, knocking over a lamp I don't care about. The wood is cold under my thighs contrasting to his body's heat and fury. His coat falls to the floor, followed by mine, a trail of tension torn loose in fabric.

My fingers knot in his shirt. He growls when I tug, pulling away just long enough to rip it off. His tattoos catch the dim light—telling stories I do not know yet, but will. His mouth finds my neck, right where that phantom bruise still sings, and I gasp.

"I remember everything," I whisper, dizzy. "Even if I wouldn't want to."

His grip tightens, his breath sharpens. I know he remembers too. His mouth drags down the line of my neck, slow and reverent, but it is the way his hands grip my thighs that undoes me—tight, grounding, trying to hold back a storm when the storm is *already* here.

I tilt my hips forward without thinking. A silent plea. His head lifts—eyes burning, jaw tight.

"You have *no* fucking idea," he rasps, breaking against my mouth, "what you do to me, to my cock."

His hands shove my skirt up, palms rough against my ass as he drags me to the border of the desk. I gasp, clutching at his shoulders while he watches every inch of my body.

"You still think this was a dream, *huh*?" he asks darkly.

I can't answer. Not when his fingers are already sliding beneath my shirt on my breast, pulling slightly my nipples.

"Because *I* did not dream it, Mira." His mouth finds my ear. "I relived it a thousand times since yesterday. Every damn second until my dick ache so badly."

A whimper catches my throat.

He lifts my chin, eyes locking with mine. "You think I can watch you walk into this place, into my world, and not lose my fucking mind?"

"Then lose it," I whisper. "Please. Lose it, Xan." I say while brushing his hair back and getting a hold of it.

He grabs me into his arms and crosses the room in seconds, laying me down on the bed with more care than I expect—the look in his eyes is anything but gentle.

His mouth crashes against mine. Every movement is frantic—needy—yet not careless. He knows my body already, somehow he memorized it the first time. I drag my nails down his back. He groans—a deep sound that makes my skin erupt in goosebumps. He bites down on my bottom lip enough to make it subtly bleed, then soothes it with his tongue as an apology.

"Xan—"

"I know." He is breathless, cracking at the precipices. "I know, baby. Just—let me."

My legs wrap around his waist, and I arch up into him, needing more—all of him inside me. The rhythm turns desperate. Beautifully unhinged. Our bodies collide over and over, until the only thing I can hear is skin, breath, the sharp drag of my name from his mouth—broken prayer.

"I waited *so* long for this," he says, forehead pressed to mine, eyes locked on mine. "So *fucking* long."

"You have me now," I breathe, my fingers tracing with reverence the part of his face he revealed just moments before, worshipping the chance to touch what he so rarely offers. "So don't you dare hold back."

That's when he loses it completely and finally pulls out his dick to trust it in one swift motion in my pussy. He growls something so guttural against my throat while penetrating me, his teeth biting deeply in my skin. My back arches off the mattress as he drives into me harder—every thrust a punishment I welcome.

"Say it," he snarls against my ear. "Say you're fucking mine."

My breath catches, but I don't hesitate. "I'm yours."

"Again."

"I'm yours, Xan. I'm—fuck—I've always been and always will."

He pins my wrists above my head with one hand, his other dragging down my thigh, branding me with every touch. His lips crush against mine again in a kiss that tastes like victory and ruin all at once.

The headboard slams against the wall. Over and over. I don't care. Let them hear. Let the whole damn Order know what he does to me—how I burn for him. How he is the only one who gets to break me.

He mutters filth between ragged breaths; words soaked in adoration. "Mine... all mine... never letting go..."

And when I shatter around him, when he follows, releasing his heat inside me with a sound I swear I never heard from anyone else—I know it.

This is not just sex. This is war.

And we have both surrendered.

Chapter 27

XAN

I sit at the brink of the bed, tightening the leather belt on my black pants. My hoodie comes next, slipping over my head as I stand and move to the single armchair stationed across the room. Mira is still on the bed, moving with that same maddening grace, pulling her shirt on clearly unaware of the way she is wrecking me.

> Try making me leave. Especially on the first night. I'm not fucking going anywhere.

I sink into the chair, spreading my legs and my arms along the worn armrests. I am claiming a throne with my phone in hand, thumb tapping out a message with a smirk tugging at my mouth.

I hit send, imagining Lucian's expression. Let him stew. Let him try. I dare him.

> I had a feeling. Do try not to wreck her too much, will you? She's got her initiation at dawn.

The Initiation.

Every soul recruited by the Order must undergo the ritual—our grim passage from hunted to hunter. We call it *The Judgment of Masks*. Archaic, maybe. Brutal, absolutely. But tradition bleeds for a reason.

Lucian will slice Mira's palm himself, right through the center as she will stand in the eye of the storm: seventeen masked members circling her like wild dogs dressed in black.

One by one, they will approach. One by one, they will press a finger to her open wound, take a single drop of her blood to their tongues, and seal her fate as one of us.

It is not just a ceremony, it's a rite. And when it is done, she will receive her mask. Her oath. Her purpose.

Then—*finally*—her training will begin. She will be assigned to missions with me, and I don't know what I am looking forward to more: watching her ascend like some sexy divine force in combat... or looking at every fool who so much as glances her way falls beneath my blade.

Either way, it is going to be a beautiful bloodbath.

As for me, I never had an initiation. No consecration. No circle. No blood-spattered welcome into the fold. I was dragged in, dropped at the doorstep like a stray, and thrown straight into work. No vows. Just orders.

However, I have watched them all since. Every single one. Year after year, I stood in that same shadowed circle, eyes sharp beneath my mask, witnessing the rebirth of the chosen few. Some trembled. Some screamed. Some smiled like they were finally home.

I did none of those things.

When I was younger, it used to gnaw at me—being the exception, the forgotten one. I would watch their blood-soaked theatrics and wonder why I was not deemed worthy of the same sacred sacrament.

But not anymore.

I have carved my worth in flesh and shadow, earned my place in silence and scars. I do not need some vampiric pageantry to remind me who the hell I am.

I *am* the ceremony they should've feared.

Somewhere between my thoughts and the slow ticking of the hour, I realize Mira has already fallen asleep.

She is sprawled across the bed without a blanket, surrendered to exhaustion—a warrior collapsing after battle. No armor. No pretense. Just raw, beautiful fatigue.

How could I blame her?

Julian's ghost still clings to her skin. The Order's burden now presses on her chest. And there is me—an entirely different kind of maelstrom she never asked for.

But damn, she wears it all like art.

I feel the weight in my eyes deepen, as if they alone have been tasked with carrying the pressure of this night all at once. The urge to resist sleep claws at me, but I know better. I will need what little rest I can steal if I am to be at my sharpest for her initiation—my beloved's first step into the dark heart of the Order.

So, I take the chair. Drag it back and plant it firmly, spine to the door. If anyone wants to come in, they will have to go through me.

Literally.

Good luck.

———— ✦ ————

In the dead hush of night, I jolt awake—heart pounding, breath caught—chased out of sleep by whispers creeping through the room.

I take a few heavy seconds to realize the voices are not foreign. They are hers.

Mira.

Still tangled in sleep, she is caught in another world, her voice soft and broken in places I have never heard before.

I rise slowly, crossing the space between us on bare feet, and lean in just enough to catch the words unraveling from her lips.

"Julian... sorry... Xan... love..."

I don't quite know what to make of it and though every part of me itches to wake her—to demand answers, to pull the truth from her mouth.

I understand. Of course I do. Regret is a natural ghost to carry after what she has been through, especially when the blood on her hands is still warm.

But she'll learn.

She will come to see that every crack I made in her world was to let the light in. That all of this—every brutal truth, every sharp twist—was to save her.

Whether or not she knows it yet.

———— 🐾 ————

I am snapped out of sleep by two harsh, echoing knocks—loud enough to make the walls flinch. I grit my teeth. Not at the sleep itself—I needed that—but at the sheer audacity of being dragged out of it.

The first thing I do is look at Mira. She is still out cold, lying sideways on the bed, hair tangled in a halo, her face soft for once. Peaceful, but not free. Not really. That piece of shit still haunts her even here, clawing at the corners of her rest.

I move the chair I had wedged against the door with slow precision, muscles tight with annoyance, keeping every sound to a minimum. No one wakes her but me.

I crack open the door just wide enough to see who thought they could knock like that and walk away untouched.

They've got three seconds to explain themselves before I stop being polite.

At the door stands a boy—sixteen, maybe seventeen at most. Still soft around the edges, all wide eyes and twitchy fingers. I swallow the urge to slam the door in his face or, better yet, break his nose clean. Because I know that look. I wore it once too, though I was half his size and twice as scared when they dragged me through these halls. He is just the messenger; a pawn caught in the turmoil of obligation.

Still, my voice comes out low and cold, laced with sleep and irritation.

"What the hell do you want?"

He freezes as if I asked him to solve a complex equation with his life on the line. His brain stalls and that is when I catch it—his gaze flickers past me, subtle as a whisper.

Not subtle enough for me.

I turn just enough to see what he is looking at.

Mira.

Fast asleep on her stomach, one leg curled up, the blanket twisted beneath her. And yeah—bare skin from her ass to her feet, glowing in the dim light, reminding a classical painting with a modern twist.

My jaw tightens.

Because now I am not just tired.

I'm fucking murderous.

I grab him by the throat and lift until he is barely grazing the floor on the tips of his toes, choking on the weight of my wrath.

"The only reason I am not gouging out your eyes right now—and believe me, I have grown quite fond of the practice, especially on men dumb enough to glance at her like she's meat—is because I know, at your age, your cock *is* your brain. I get it. I have been there. Alone, desperate, stuck in these walls long enough and even the curve of a chair leg starts looking seductive."

I lean in, voice velvet and violence.

"But don't you *ever* look at my little fox like that again. In fact—don't look at any woman that fucking creepy way. Because I swear to every dark god that has ever heard a prayer—your dick will be your next meal."

The boy immediately lowers his head, hands trembling as he offers me a bundle of white, slightly sheer fabric.

"What exactly am I supposed to do with this?" I ask flatly.

He stammers, voice barely audible. "The Ruler... he asked me to bring this... for your roommate's initiation... sir."

My brow lifts. "Roommate?" I echo, venom threading through the word.

"Never refer to Mira as anything other than mine. Are we clear?"

He nods so fast I am surprised his head does not fall off, dropping the fabric into my hands before practically sprinting away.

"Hey!" I call after him. He halts mid-escape. "What's your name, kid?"

"O-... Owen, sir. Can I ask... why?" I smirk, clearly amused.

"So I can give it to Mira when she wakes. Let her decide your horrible fate herself."

The boy gives me a frantic nod—his silent, terrified vow he understands, accepts his destiny, and possibly his doom. What he does not know is that I have no intention of saying a damn thing to Mira. But the fear alone should serve as a lifelong lesson. I chuckle quietly, amused by the absurd threat I just made.

For a split second—one dangerous, flickering second—I catch myself thinking: if I'd had a father, maybe that is the kind of joke he would have made. The kind of half-violent, half-affectionate lesson a man passes down when he wants to scare you straight, yet still lets you laugh through the trauma.

Then it hits me—maybe that is exactly the father I would be. The kind who growls, threatens, makes boys tremble in doorways, all in the name of protecting what is his. And I don't know if that is comforting or horrifying. Probably both. But no child deserves to be a mirror of me.

290

That thought alone is enough to strangle the fantasy at the root. I shove it out of my mind, lock the door behind me, and return to the only thing that matters: *her.*

Before waking my girl up, I take a moment to unfold the sheer bundle of fabric the boy nearly died delivering. Turns out, it is a gown—well, barely. A plunging neckline, a dripping collar of lace, and a train long enough to make Rapunzel consider a haircut.

I have never witnessed a woman's initiation before. Apparently, there is a dress code—and it is one gust of wind away from indecency. I am not exactly thrilled about the transparency. The idea of anyone else seeing what is mine makes my jaw ache, but I swore I would not make this day about me.

Today is *hers* only.

And I promised myself I would try just for once, to keep my guard down to a level slightly below feral.

"Morning, little fox. Go ahead—take a minute to wake up and let it sink in: this is not just a dream today either."

Her lashes lift. That half-asleep glow in her eyes flickers to life the second she sees me. One hand finds its way into my hair.

"I wouldn't trade this dream for anything," she whispers.

I smirk, a little too proud of myself. "You're cheesy."

She grins, sleep-drunk and smug. "Obviously."

I am starting to think I am the one still dreaming—because finding love like this, and worse, getting to keep it within the walls of the Order, feels like something out of a twisted fairytale. I used to believe I was built to be alone forever, cycling through fleeting conquests like empty glasses at the end of a long night. But no. Somehow, against all odds, even Xan Hayes gets a shot at happiness... as dark and bloodstained as it may be.

Chapter 28

MIRA

I wake up for the second time, startled by how safe I feel despite everything. Xan had woken me earlier, whispering about needing to check on something, and promised he would be back soon. I must have mumbled a response, still tangled in sleep, because the next thing I knew, I was drifting off again, lulled by the soft echo of his voice and the fading scent of him in the room. Now, with the light filtering through the heavy curtains and brushing against my skin, I know it is time.

I sit up; the sheets falling away, and I catch sight of a robe. *The* robe. It is draped over the chair like some sort of ceremonial threat, delicate and sheer, with a neckline so low it practically introduces itself before I even put it on and a train long enough to drown a girl if she wasn't careful. A dress you wear when you are about to be reborn—or sacrificed.

Part of me wants to laugh—nervous, borderline hysterical—but another part feels oddly calm.

Because I know he will be there.

If he can survive this world with his heart still beating, then maybe... so can I.

I notice there is a note—small, folded, sitting on top of the desk.

Back soon. Don't be late for your own legend. X -

I smile despite the chill in the room. The bastard knows exactly what to say to twist a knot in my stomach. I rise slowly, legs tangled in the sheets, body sore in the best possible way. My fingers graze once again on the gown that was left behind.

It is... stunning. Barely there. Ethereal, something worn by the ghost of a goddess. I lift it in front of me, eyeing the delicate train and neckline that dips low enough to challenge modesty itself.

Was this really for an initiation—or a date?

Either way, I know I am wearing it. I know I am walking out of this room with my head high, even if I do not know what today holds.

I slip into the dress carefully, almost reverently. It feels like stepping into another skin—one I am not sure I have earned yet, but one that somehow fits like fate. My curves are barely concealed, but I do not shy away from my reflection. Not today.

Today, I become someone else. Or maybe... more of who I have always been.

I tame my hair with my fingers, then find a small clasp left on the dresser—a silver pin in the shape of a fox. A gift from *him*, I suppose. I slide it into place, just above my ear. For the first time in days, I smile at myself.

When I open the door, the hallway outside is quiet, but there is energy in the air—a thunder waiting just behind the clouds. I have no idea where I am going, not exactly. But I know who I'm looking for. And when I find Xan again, I will be walking toward my future—with blood in my veins, fire in my chest, and a name the Order will never forget.

Just as I am about to take another step down the hall, a soft knock interrupts the silence behind me. I turn. Standing in the hallway is a boy—barely sixteen. He is all nerves and too-big clothes, clutching a black envelope like it is ticking in his hands.

"Miss Vale...?" he asks, voice cracking halfway through.

I nod slowly.

"I have been sent to escort you... to the Rite."

The way he says it—with a capital R. It is holy and dangerous all at once.

He does not meet my eyes. His gaze flickers briefly to the floor, then to the folds of my dress, and instantly back down again, cheeks reddening like he has been caught looking at a goddess he does not feel worthy of worship.

"Lead the way," I say softly as I watch the tension in his shoulders ease just a little.

While I follow him, barefoot down a marble corridor, I realize this is it. The moment between the before and the after.

Somewhere near to here, Xan is waiting for my ascension.

The boy—Owen, as he had introduced himself, guides me through the bowels of the Order in near-total silence. The hallways we pass feel older than time, mounted with obsidian stone that drinks in the flickering light of the wall sconces. His footsteps are soft—the kind that suggest even the floor might punish him for stepping too loudly. I try to match his pace. Every echo of my bare feet against the cold stone floor feels amplified, a scream in the silence.

Eventually, we stop before a pair of massive double doors— twice my height, sculpted in ancient black oak, their surface etched with archaic runes and twisting symbols that seem to writhe and shimmer in the candlelight. The handles are forged from wrought iron, each one a curved dagger frozen midstrike.

Owen turns to me, wide-eyed and pale, his Adam's apple bobbing as he swallows.

"This is where I leave you," he whispers, anything louder might summon a demon best left sleeping. "They are waiting inside."

I nod, though my chest is tightening.

"Good luck... Miss Vale," he adds, barely louder than the breath it took to speak it. And just like that, he vanishes, swallowed by the shadows behind us.

I linger for a moment; hand poised above the dagger handle. The wood radiates heat, or maybe it's my pulse surging in my fingertips. I close my eyes.

One breath.

Another.

Then I push.

The doors creak open with the groan of an ancient beast, revealing a vast circular chamber bathed in candlelight. The ceiling soars above me in a dome of stone and colored glass, where stained panels filter the waning morning sun into fractured shards of gold and crimson. Smoke coils like silk through the air, rising from censers, hung at regular intervals around the room. It smells of myrrh and burnt cedar.

Seventeen figures form a ring around the center, unmoving, cloaked in silence. Every one of them is dressed in robes as black as oil and wears a mask as dark as pitch—sleek, smooth, anonymous. A council of phantoms.

At the center stands Lucian Voss.

He is dressed in ceremonial black, a subtle sheen in the fabric that catches the light like liquid ink. His mask, sculpted from silver steel, devours every glint that touches it. There is a stillness to him that is more than human. It is the silence of the executioner before the blade falls.

This is it.

The Judgement of the Masks.

I scan the room, eyes darting from one masked figure to the next, desperate to spot Xan among the sea of identical shadows. I thought it would be easy—how many men could possibly share his height, that sinful broadness of shoulder? Apparently, at least eight. Eight!

My heart clenches with growing panic. I *know* he is here—he *must* be—but the fact that I cannot pinpoint him sends a wave of irrational dread crawling up my back. It is like playing *Where's Waldo* in a cultist's surreal haze.

A deep, echoing gong shatters the silence. In eerie unison, every masked figure stomps their right foot against the ground. The sound reverberates—thunder trapped in a crypt. Odd, sure—but at this point, the least strange thing in all of this might just be the door handles, even if they look like something straight out of Satan's interior designer's catalog.

I notice, at the center of the room, directly across from Lucian, stands a strange ancient-looking altar made of stone. With a slow, sweeping motion of his hand, he gestures for me to approach. I hesitate, scanning again the sea of masked faces for any trace of Xan. A twitch of a finger, a tilt of a shoulder— anything to ground me. Yet nothing. Just black masks and quiet.

Swallowing my nerves, I draw in a shaky breath and step forward. The slab is cold and imposing, clearly stolen straight from some sacrificial temple. Graceful as a newborn giraffe, I climb up onto the massive stone and lie down, trying not to think about how this feels less like a rite of passage and more like the start of *The Shining*, minus the snow.

Now lying flat—on what might generously be described as *slightly more comfortable than a deflated camping mattress*, I stare up at the vaulted ceiling, trying not to shiver.

Lucian steps into view, shrouded in shadow, his silver mask glinting like the blade of a guillotine. His theatrical voice cuts through the mute calm.

"Today, the Order parts its impenetrable gates for fresh blood. May the assassinations be many and the chaos of life cling relentlessly to our newest sister, Mira Vale."

Of course. Nothing says *"welcome"* like ceremonial bloodletting and a death wish disguised as a blessing.

The seventeen masked members strike the floor with their right heels in unison again, the sound echoing, a war drum pounding through the chamber.

Then, in perfect synchronicity, they all turn their backs to me. Alright. Weird flex, but okay.

Lucian steps forward, drawing his ceremonial dagger—curved, ornate, and unnecessarily ominous. I extend my hand, expecting the classic palm cut Xan had warned me about. You know, simple. Manageable. Symbolic.

But no.

Lucian's masked face tilts slightly, and instead of slashing my hand, he guides the blade higher. Much higher. The point of the dagger rests just beneath my sternum—dead center. Before I can react, he presses.

The knife punctures the skin with brutal elegance, sliding into the soft flesh between my ribs. The pain is immediate and white-hot, blooming through my chest with such precision it feels as though it pierces straight into my heart.

I wonder if this was it—if I was truly about to die here, carved open like a pig on this cold slab of stone. I suddenly feel the blade glide downward, dragging a searing line from my chest to just above my navel. Then... he pulls it out, smooth as silk.

Okay. Cool. Guess I'm *not* dying. Not yet anyway.

He wipes the blade with a length of black satin, like it has its own sacred ritual and not just him cleaning up my insides. With all the ceremony of a twisted tailor, he lays the dagger beside me—perfectly parallel to my hips.

With a strange sort of care, he lifts the blood-stained tissue and wraps it around my eyes. The fabric sticks to my skin, warm and damp. I can smell the iron instantly—so strong I can even taste it. It fills my mouth, my nose, my throat, until I feel like I am breathing it in.

The slash across my stomach burns like acid—sharp and far too real—still my mind barely registers it. Everything is buzzing, hazy. My brain is trying to buffer through a hallucinatory fever blur. The ache is there, screaming, but it is drowned out by the intensity of the moment, by the blood, the whispers, the goddamn satin caging my sight.

Lucian's voice cuts through the silence like a chef master announcing dinner service at Hell's five-star resort.

"Let the feast begin. Try to savor boys—gluttony leaves such a mess."

Charming. Just what you want to hear when your guts are barely staying in place.

I hear the first set of footsteps pivot behind me as one of the masked members steps forward to the altar. My nerves spike so violently, my soul seems to push itself out of my body. I feel myself drifting, detaching—floating somewhere above the stone slab like some desperate guardian angel watching the scene unfold.

The problem is, the poor soul splayed out on the altar below, stripped of sight and sanity, blood seeping down her side... is me. And all I want to do is scream at this invisible version of myself: *run, girl—get off the damn table.*

But I can't. I am completely incapable of moving, of fleeing, of doing anything other than lying here as some tragic offering. I must go through with this. Not just for Xan—even if the thought of him is anchoring—but for me. For the version of Mira that is clawing her way out of the ashes of the girl I used to be.

That old version? She is fucking gone. Buried somewhere beneath heartbreak, fury, and a stone altar slick with her own blood. What is rising now... is something else entirely.

Though I cannot see a damn thing, I feel someone standing over me. The air shifts—heavier, colder—and, without warning, a finger presses into the fresh wound on my abdomen.

A choked gasp escapes me. The pain is blinding—sharp and searing, a molten blade shoved straight into my gut. My back arches instinctively against the stone beneath me, trapped in stillness, strapped down—not by force, now by fear.

Every nerve in my body screams. It burns, it throbs, it boils. I clench my jaw, already dreading the fact that this was only the first... one down, *sixteen* to go. Sixteen more men. Sixteen more hands. Sixteen more trials by stirring fire.

If I survive until number five, I am convinced my insides are going to just spill out onto the floor like overcooked spaghetti. Yet—I stay. I endure. Because this is not just suffering.

It is the price of becoming someone no one will ever dare to touch without my permission again.

And comes the next one. Another faceless shadow stepping forward to take their turn. I brace myself, even if it is useless. The pain hits again—sharp and invasive—like the first time.

I keep waiting for the adrenaline to kick in, to work its magic and numb the agony. Isn't that how this is supposed to go? Body in shock, mind floating away somewhere safer?

Sadly, my body is clearly too stubborn, or too aware. Every nerve is awake, on high alert. The sting does not dull at all—it multiplies, spreads. I am starting to think I will feel every goddamn one of them as if it was the first. Again and again.

When the next figure approaches, I count—*eleven*. This is the eleventh one. Which means there are only six more to go. Just six. I cannot believe it. The end is finally creeping closer.

For a moment, I genuinely thought Julian's murder would be the peak of my life's trauma chart. Like the defining moment of unbearable horror.

But *oh*, how naïve of me.

Life—or rather, the Order—had other plans. Apparently, rock bottom has a basement. Here I am, spread out on a stone altar, bleeding, blindfolded, and being sampled like an hors d'oeuvre at a cannibalistic wine tasting.

And this man... this man takes his time. Excruciatingly so. I can hear his breath hitch as he leans closer, inhaling me like a dying deer, catching the scent of salvation. He finally exhales. A low, guttural sigh of satisfaction that snakes down my spine like liquid heat.

That is when I know.

It's him. It has to be. The man standing over me, the only one reckless enough to savor this moment in the middle of a ritual soaked in blood and madness... is Xan.

His finger—god, his delightful finger—trails across my skin with agonizing patience, leaving fire in its wake. I shudder, the tremor starting at my scalp and rippling all the way down between my thighs, helpless to the way my body reacts to him, even now, especially now.

He draws a path along the dip of my collarbone while his presence devours me in silence. Every inch of contact with a slow-burning brand. He is trying to remind me who I belong to without saying a damn thing.

I feel his breath first, a predator savoring every heartbeat of the moment—warm and maddening—ghosting between the curve of my breasts. Then come the kisses.

He trails them down the center of my chest following a sacred map etched into my torso, and each one ignites a spark that threatens to set my entire soul in flame. My breath catches when he pauses just above the cut—my wound, my offering, my curse—I swear time halts with him.

He kisses there, right above the place where the pain still lingers. It is gentle, a twisted apology wrapped in affection. I do not know whether to cry or laugh or drag him up by the collar and scream at him for making me feel so much while I am still blindfolded and bleeding.

Of course it is Xan.

Only he would think this was the time for tenderness. Only he would make the abyss feel like home.

As he reaches the beginning of my wound, I feel it—his tongue. Warm. Slow. Sinfully deliberate dipping into the open slit of my skin, tasting divinity itself.

A sound escapes me. Barely audible, involuntary—and it yanks me out of the daze he is pulling me into.

What the hell is happening to me?

I can feel him—quite *literally*—drinking me from the inside out. The sensation is, without question, the strangest thing I have ever experienced... yet, somehow, it is also one of the most devastatingly satisfying. It is like every nerve in my core has been rewired to worship him at this exact moment.

There is no metaphor left—I am giving myself to him, blood, body, and soul. No games, no illusions. Just me, laid bare and bleeding on a slab of ancient rock with him feasting on my surrender.

A part of me never wants this euphoric ritual to end. God help me, all I want right now is to grab his hand and take him back to my room like some delirious lunatic, just so he can show me what else that sinful tongue of his is capable of.

If it can turn agony into pleasure with nothing but a flick against torn flesh, I can only fantasize about what it does when the stakes are not about knives and ceremony, but lust and indulgence.

Forget demonic rites and hard stones—I want soft sheets, locked doors, and his mouth tracing paths that have everything to do with pure desire. I want to trade the chill of this boulder for the burn of his skin against mine.

His mouth finds the hollow of my throat, tongue tracing slow, possessive patterns as though he is branding me with every stroke. I arch beneath him, helpless against the ache building in my pussy. My breath stutters when he bites down, just hard enough, and I swear I could unravel from that alone.

His hand tightens around my chest, teasing, wanting to hear me beg. Geez, I might. The warmth of his breath against my skin is unbearable, each exhale a whisper of promise I am desperate to believe. I do not know if I want him to stop or to ruin me completely. Maybe both. Maybe that is the point.

He dips lower, dangerously close to the place Lucian carved into me, and I brace myself for another taste of that torturous euphoria.

However, the moment his tongue brushes against my wound again, a low, mocking chuckle escapes his mask. It is subtle—barely more than a breath—but it coils through the air like smoke and freezes something in me.

That laugh... it's wrong. Too smug. Too self-satisfied.

A slow dread crawls up my spine. The sound does not match Xan—there is no warmth in it, no reverence. It is only cruel.

My breath hitches.

Oh my God.

That is not him. That is not *my* monster.

Whoever it is, he is enjoying this way too much.

The hand on my breast grows rougher, more mechanical, squeezing as if testing ripeness. My body lights up in a surge of raw, red flares.

This is officially not Xan.

The pressure of the glove shifts, and there is no warmth left. No pulse. Just cold leather and a stranger's breath, panting hard against my stomach, my pain fueling him. My chest tightens as panic claws its way through the haze of heat and confusion.

That delicious, dangerous thrill was not desire. It was deceit. The man consuming me—the one I had given myself to in blind devotion—is not Xan.

It's Kayde.

And he has been feasting on me, devouring what was never meant to be his.

I try to sit up, but the searing burn in my abdomen reminds me in the cruelest way that my stomach has been deliberately split open like a sacrificial fruit. I'm trapped. Pinned by pain, by fear, by the horrifying realization that I am not in control of a single goddamn thing. Terror crawls up my spine, wraps around my throat, and squeezes.

Desperate, I tear off the blindfold, my fingers shaking, slick with sweat and blood. I wish I hadn't. Hovering just inches above my face stands a masked demon. It stares down at me with a tilt of amusement, watching me squirm beneath its gaze, a trapped insect under glass. There is no mercy in those eyes. Just... hunger. And devastating delight.

As if the horror was not enough, he lifts a gloved finger to his mouth and makes a soft, slow shushing motion—*shhh*. My blood runs cold. My breath catches mid-scream. I am paralyzed. Not by his face, but by the sick pleasure curling at the corners of his hidden grin.

God, I want Xan to turn around.

To just feel it—some strange, cosmic pull in his gut that screams something is wrong. I want him to shatter the silence. To break rank. To come storming through this ritual like some furious dark knight and rip the wolf right off my body with those blood-stained hands of his.

Sadly, nothing.

No hint of that wild instinct he always seems to have when it comes to me.

I guess—for once in his entire maddening, defiant existence—Xan Hayes has decided to follow the rules.

And I have never hated obedience more in my goddamn life.

"Please... stop, Kayde," I whisper, my voice barely audible—meant for him and him alone. "I belong to Xan. And you know damn well that the moment he finds out what you did to me... He is going to tear you apart."

I can see the glint of silver in Kayde's eyes narrowing behind his mask—a cruel smile practically bleeding through his voice as he lets out a soft, mocking laugh.

"You know, Mira," he murmurs, tilting his head with theatrical pity, "Xan will not always be there to swoop in and save his little damsel. Sooner or later, you will have to learn how to stand on your own... big girl boots and all."

His hand snakes down, fingers tracing the inside of my thigh with an infuriating slowness, and I shudder against my will.

"From where I'm standing," he whispers, leaning closer until I can feel his breath, "you didn't seem upset at all earlier. In fact... I would wager you might be a little curious what it is like when the wrong man touches you just right."

My hand lashes out before I even register the decision—a brutal slap cracks through the thick, suffocating silence of the chamber. The sound echoes like a gunshot, yet his head barely turns from the impact. Instead, I watch his chest rise with the fury that coils before it strikes.

In one swift motion, his gloved hand closes around my throat, ice-cold and merciless. He lifts me effortlessly, my back arching as the pressure tightens. My legs scramble against the altar for leverage, for air—for anything. Panic surges as I claw at his grip, the edges of my vision fuzzing while I gasp, desperate to reclaim the breath his wrath is stealing from me.

Just as my eyes roll back, the whites taking over like a curtain call on my consciousness, I feel Kayde's grip suddenly vanish. My body drops like a dead weight off the altar, hitting the floor with a sickening thud. The jagged rim scrapes down my leg, tearing my skin wide open, but I am too dazed to scream.

I gasp, every inhale a struggle, forcing my eyes to open just enough to catch a glimpse—not of Kayde's triumphant face above me, but of... nothing. Just the rumble of something crashing behind me. The heavy sound of a human crumpling.

I don't know what just happened. However, for the first time since this nightmare began, I am not the only one bleeding.

It's in that moment—through the haze of pain and panic—that I see him.

Xan.

Standing tall and breathless over Kayde's twitching, crumpled body. In his hand, gripped tightly, is what looks like the shattered remains of an antique plaster statue, white dust still drifting from the impact.

I want to run to him, throw myself into his arms, bury my face in his neck and cling to him. He is the only solid thing left in a world that is falling apart.

I want to thank him over and over, kiss him until the pandemonium melts away—until I can believe I am safe. Nonetheless, my body won't move. It is nailed to the ground.

That's when I feel it—the hot, sticky warmth pooling beneath me. The edges of my vision blur, and a cold realization settles in my chest: I am losing too much blood.

If I do not hold on... I might not make it long enough to tell him how much I needed him.

Everything feels so... far away.

Muted. Like I am watching myself from somewhere else, floating just above this bleeding, broken corpse...

"Fuck, Mira!"

His voice slices through the. Xan falls to his knees beside me, and suddenly, the world crashes back into focus—all just agony and trembling limbs.

I blink slowly, barely able to move my head. At least I can see him.

The way his hands hover inches above my body, terrified to hurt me more. The frantic way his chest rises and falls, like he has forgotten how to breathe. The way he whispers my name again and again, as if it is both a question and a plea.

"Mira... no. No, no—please!"

His voice breaks. Not cracks. *Breaks* as his entire soul is crumbling from the inside out.

I want to reach for him. I want to tell him I am still here—*barely*, but here. My lips are too dry, my throat too raw, and the blood loss has turned my limbs to stone. I can feel it leaving me.

Life. Warmth. Color.

My fingers twitch. That's all I can manage. It is enough to catch his attention. His eyes meet mine through the holes in his mask.

A mask I have seen in dreams, in nightmares, in memories I tried to bury.

This time though... he looks scared. Not for himself. For me. His whole body is shaking now.

"Don't—don't do this to me, baby," he cries. "I'm here. I'm here, little fox—just stay with me. Please, fuck!"

I realize the cold. The slipping.

Air barely comes. My vision darkens around the sides. I cannot hold on much longer. The panic wells up in my chest like a tidal wave that never breaks.

"I..." I breathe, lips barely moving. "I don't want to die, Xan."

He freezes.

For one heartbeat—maybe two—he does not move at all. Then slowly, shakily, Xan reaches for his mask. His fingers hesitate.

He is afraid.

Afraid of what I'll see.

Afraid that it is too late.

Afraid that if he takes it off, this moment will be too real.

With a shuddering exhale, he pulls the mask from his face.

I finally see him.

His hair is wild, damp with sweat and speckled in blood. His jaw is clenched like it's the only thing holding him together. And his eyes—God, his eyes—are gorgeously devastated.

There is a tear trailing down his cheek, carving a path through the dirt and blood like it has nowhere else to go. He looks at me as if he is watching the sun die.

"Mira... I love you."

It is not a declaration. It is a surrender. A truth he has held for too long. It lands between us with the weight of everything we never said.

I try to answer. I try so hard. Instead, I give him the only thing I have left—my gaze.

Full of everything I did not get to say.

My apology.

My goodbye.

My *love*.

I look at him.

One last time.

His face swimming in tears and horror and desperate, desperate love.

To nothing.

The world slips from beneath me like sand between fingers, and all that remains is silence.

But somewhere—in that last, flickering second—I hold onto that voice.

That whisper.

That vow.

Mira... I love you.

The End.

Huge thanks to my loving husband, who gifted me a shiny new computer and bravely endured every wild idea, half-baked script, and downright weird proposal I threw his way. You're not just perfect—you're my personal hero in this chaotic creative mess.

To my wonderful kids, who didn't lose their minds yelling, "Mom, you're still glued to that laptop!" every five seconds. Your patience is legendary and I love you so freaking much.

To my friend Vicky, who somehow survived 4,893,298 cover art disasters without disowning me. Seriously, you deserve a medal, some things were very ugly.

To my Alpha, Beta, and ARC readers—without your brutally honest feedback, I'd probably still be lost in chapter one.

To the *Dark Romance Book Club* on Facebook, they hooked me up with some great Alpha, Beta, and ARC readers who kept me rolling. Couldn't have gotten this far without you guys.

And to *The Office* and *World of Warcraft*—my only lifelines, my sanity savers, my reasons to believe the world is slightly less messed up than my manuscript.

www.ingramcontent.com/pod-product-compliance
Lightning Source LLC
Chambersburg PA
CBHW070847260626
47170CB00007B/2528